Lady

Starling's

Stockings

By Cerise DeLand

For Steve

Lady Starling's Stockings

Chapter One

Naples, Italy

September 30, 1815

Lady Solange Starling adjusted her mask and gazed out over the assemblage at the British Embassy, searching the ballroom with a blasé smile—and a determination fraught with frustration.

Where, oh, where are you, Monsieur? Dinner is done, the dancing about to begin and I am bursting with news and questions!

Among the pale flocks of British ladies and somber olive-skinned Italian matrons, Solange wove her way through the throng to find her contact. Out of courtesy, she had to stop here and there often to permit the gentlemen who came to her to kiss her hand, murmur greetings and attempt to charm her. Despite her ostrich-feathered mask, these diplomats and naval officers, both English and Italian, knew her curvaceous figure, her love of fashion—and her noble English name. They knew she was wealthy and half French. And all that they knew of her came from two sources—her reign over the *ton* in London as Lord George Starling's young bride and his widow, plus her previous visit here at the embassy to her cousin and his wife. On Solange's first sojourn to Naples three months ago, she had accomplished her mission to find the traitor who turned out to be her cousin's naval adjutant. And she had done it within days of sailing into port.

Now, given the threatened return of Napoleon's brother-in-law Murat here to reclaim his throne of Naples, her newest task was greater and more urgent. And my contact? *Monsieur de la Guerre? Where is he?*

"My lady, Solanj-a," the Neapolitan prince of D'oro crooned to her in his heavily accented English. "I am so happy to see you have returned to us here in Napoli."

"*Va bene*, Your Highness, how could I stay away?" She flirted with the eagle-eyed naval officer, using a gay tilt to her head and a flash of her silver blue eyes. A man notorious for his spendthrift ways and his frequent bouts with the pox, Prince Giorgio peered at her with a salacious intensity before letting his gaze scan down her figure.

"Have you had the opportunity to shop yet in the main piazza, *cara mia*?"

"You remember well my little amusement to keep my modiste rapidly sewing, dear Prince." Ignoring his rudeness to address her so casually, she pursed her lips and allowed him to savor the sight of them.

"I wish to learn more about you than your preference for the richest fabrics, my lovely bird," he said, his tongue sliding across his lower lip.

"Now, now," she teased him, tapping her fan to his arm and walking toward the terrace. She led this man on as she did all men. She had no one in her bed. Had invited no one since her elderly husband passed on to his grave reward five years ago. And though she longed for a spectacular lover to fill her body and obsess her mind, she had spotted no candidates who matched her ideals. Until such a specimen of manhood appeared and could match one unforgettable champion she'd met half a lifetime ago, she would remain alone in her bed by night and at her espionage by day. "Though I confess, I would love to shop for a few yards of Venetian lace."

"For a camisole?" he asked, his gaze afire with hunger. "Do you need one? As creamy as your skin? I will order one made!"

"You are too kind. I would not trouble you. But alas, I am so occupied, Your Highness. You must have heard it said about that I did come this time to help my cousin's wife after her recent lying-in."

"You should have a child of your own." He grabbed her hand. His own was clammy, and Solange bore with the cool sweat like a seasoned soldier of the Cold Stream Guard. "You are so lovely, so well formed...what is the English word? Endowed? I am certain God has blessed you with the ability to bear many children, *bella mia*." His thin black brows wiggled high while he circled her waist and pressed his fingers to the side of her breast.

She smiled serenely at him, the lascivious cuss. Then she picked up her pace. She would tempt him, but she would not bed him. Her stock in trade was her own sensual allure. Without her golden looks and her acute perception, without her sloe-eyed sensuality that she never tamped, she would not have become one of Home Office's most accomplished spies. She enjoyed the chase and she would not stop intriguing men. Not now. Not when victory over the last of that tyrant Bonaparte's men was soon to come. Not when that victory depended on her rooting out the French operative who had burrowed himself so deeply into her cousin's diplomatic staff that he threatened the peace of Europe with his nefarious presence. "You are too complimentary, Your Highness."

"Never! Beauty such as yours blossoms, I am certain, when a seasoned lover teaches you the delights you so richly deserve."

Forward fart.

"I would show you my newest mill. On the road to Roma." They descended the terrace steps, and Solange purposely stopped at the entrance to the maze. She would not offer him any solitude in which to accost her. "I purchased it two weeks ago."

"So recently?" She marveled that these Neapolitans changed sides so easily. "Are you not concerned that Murat's spies lurk on the road to Rome?"

"Murat has lost all friends among us. He is a nasty cat, one day with his brother-in-law, one day with the Austrians and you British. Forget politics, lovely Solanj-a. Come with me in my carriage to view my fabrics."

"Ah, Your Highness, tempting surely." To go out with this lecher alone in his carriage would cause all kinds of a scandal. Yet Solange needed to discover if Giorgio was simply dedicated to her seduction or if he wished to glean information about her cousin and the British naval blockade of the city. After all, Giorgio had been a close friend of the naval attaché whom she had put to ground three months ago. Plus she had seen Giorgio only an hour ago in hot discussion in one corner with a French émigré whom she suspected of collusion with the Bonapartists. "But you know I must not disappear with you alone. My family, my friends. Why, you must imagine how they would view an afternoon with you." She widened her eyes and consoled him with a tiny moue.

"Bring your maid, if you must," he told her, opening his mouth and coming so close she smelled the garlic and onions of his lunch.

Oh, *merde.* "A charming solution!" She tried not to wince—or inhale the fumes.

"I will show you silk such as you have never seen."

Silk? Her favorite. Her fetish.

"From Lucca's finest worms."

"Luccan silk." She repeated like a half-wit. Luccan silk. Reputed to be made from Chinese worms given by Kublai Khan to Marco Polo. "I have never felt it."

"I will allow you to feel everything." He grasped her hands and in his rabid desire, squeezed the blood out of them. "Everything!"

His innuendo was not lost on her. She grimaced, surrendering to her need to investigate his life further.

"Well, Your Highness, I–"

"I will give you all you need, Solanj-a. My silks. More. Come with me for the day, the night–"

A man coughed. Once. Twice. From behind the tall cypresses.

Giorgio's heavy brows darted together. At once, he hauled her against his wiry body and his very rigid cock. "Ignore him, *bella*. Tell me you will come–"

Solange stepped backward. How to deter him politely from handling her like a whore, hmmm?

He took no heed, but flowed toward her, pressing his mouth to her ear–and his lips were as wet as his hands. "I am mad for you, my lovely English lady."

From behind the tall evergreen next to them, a gentleman cleared his throat.

Their interloper's intrusions made her suppress a chuckle. "Your Highness, your offer of the afternoon–"

"Your offer, Your Highness," a booming bass voice surrounded Solange like a villain in a Venetian opera as a man strolled from the bushes, "is wonderful. The lady will consider it and write you tomorrow with her answer."

Solange stared up at the towering figure before her. Taller than most men she'd met. More fit, as well. Dressed entirely in black, save for his flowing white stock, he looked like a devil's disciple. Even to his rich ebony hair that fell over his brow and the large black velvet mask that covered his eyes and cheeks but not his strong square jaw.

"And who are you to speak for the lady, sir?" Giorgio asked, his lips curled in outrage at this interference.

"I am an old friend of hers from her childhood," the apparition in midnight hues responded with derision. "I am certain she remembers me. Don't you, *ma cherie*?"

Solange swayed on her feet, her forehead cool, her eyes burning with the sight of the man she had wished to return to her, lo, these fifteen years. Even now, as Giorgio stormed off, she was blinded by brilliant memories from her wretched past.

Grinning like a satyr, her man in black swept her into his arms and carried her to a nook in the maze. There he sat upon a small stone settee and plopped her on his lap.

"I have shocked you," he said with soothing strokes of the back of his hand to her forehead and her cheeks. "I meant to be more gallant and introduce myself in a civil manner in the ballroom. But that man intruded. He irritates me to no end."

She caught her breath, her gaze all over this man whose face she saw within her shattered memories of her parents, Paris and the trumbulls. "Me, too," she admitted because she knew she could speak to this man plainly as she could no other. "How did you find me? Why...here? Why now?"

He eyes sparked with humor. They were black, brilliant and bold. "I am here to help you, my dear Solange."

Help? Do what? Why would the man who as a youth had once pulled her from the dastardly cart headed for the guillotine appear now? After years in which she thought him dead, how could he help her? He would probably faint if he knew what she did for her adopted country. And for that, she did not require his help but her dear *Monsieur de la Guerre's*.

This led her to the more pertinent question. "Where the hell have you been all these years?"

"Shh. That will come." He glanced this way and that to check the entrances to the maze. Then he turned the full magnetic power of those onyx eyes on her. "I have been in Naples for three months."

"Three—?" *Since I first came here?* "Since Murat left with the remnants of his army and his pride?"

His long lashes lowered in a sign of agreement. "I'm here to help you, *ma cherie*. With your work."

My work, she mouthed. Then narrowed her eyes on him. Her investigative work?

He nodded, then whispered. "I am your new contact."

"Why?" she shot back, beneath her breath.

"You can guess the sad cause, my pet." His gem-like eyes spoke of death.

"No." She shook her head, disbelieving his implication. "*Monsieur de la Guerre?*"

He set his jaw.

She shot to her feet. Fluttered her fan. Turned this way and that as she swallowed her tears. If her *Monsieur* was dead, then the cause could surely be put to his carelessness. Or was it my own? "How?"

"I cannot tell you here."

She stomped her foot. "You must."

"Have a care, Solange."

"Name a place. A time. And how do you know this in any case?" Was she a fool to trust a man she had not seen in fifteen years? Much had changed since last he had rescued her from one of Napoleon's agents when she was fifteen. Even more since his first rescue of her when both of them were prisoners of the Committee of Public Safety, condemned to be murdered by the Parisian mob. "And how do you know this about my *Monsieur?*"

"I have friends," he told her beneath his breath. He rose and once more, his imperial height took her breath and filled her vision with his masterly command. Over the intervening years, he had matured from gangly youth to vigorous compelling manhood. His warm hands cupped her elbows as he drew so near she felt once more the life-giving warmth of his body.

Once he had cradled her like this, sheltered her from angry churls who sought to kill them both. Once he had hid her in gutted, charred *chateaux* and foresters' shacks. Once he had dug potatoes from ravaged earth for their suppers. He'd caught rabbits, skinned them, roasted them over fires, and thereby kept them both from starvation. Once he had helped her stow away from Calais to Dover and set them both free of Robespierre. He had drawn her close then, kept her warm, fed and told her tales to make her believe that one day all strife, all war, all useless killing would end. In some ways, he had been right.

But in most, he had been wrong. If she was grateful to him for having saved her even as he saved himself, she was also cognizant that if the world was to be free of tyrants, then she must help ensure it. And so she had done for the past four years with what weapons she possessed. Her beauty, her brains and her courage. "Come, Solange. Know that my work complements your own. I will tell you about this, but at a better place and time."

"Then call on me tomorrow here at noon."

"I cannot."

"Of course, you can."

"I am known here."

"And not welcome?" Had he changed loyalties over the past years? She could not imagine it. Yet, it might have occurred. "Why would my cousin James refuse you?"

"James? No." He flourished a hand to denote his mask. "But others? *Oui*, there are more, Solange."

"In the house? Here? Oh, damn it, man! What do you know?"

He stepped back and shot his cuffs. "You and I will meet. Soon."

She blinked. "Where?"

He chuckled, a rich sound of hilarity. "When it is possible, I shall send you word."

She stepped closer, enough to inhale the lemon and sandalwood of his soap. Her throat constricting with the heady fragrance, she whispered, "I do not like surprises."

"How well I recall." He took a step toward the house, but turned to look into her eyes with solemn purpose. "I will send a well-penned note."

She stilled. 'A well-penned note.' The code for a transmission of import. He knew this secret set of passwords. Which meant he was most definitely a British spy. And that's how he came to know of *Monsieur de la Guerre's* demise. Her reluctance to counter him crumpled and she gave him the appropriate response, "I am eager to read it."

"Until then, be vigilant. Careful."

She rushed to him, her fingers clutching his frock coat, the superfine beneath her skin warm with his body heat. She should be rejoicing in his very existence, not questioning his methods to suppressing the same tyrants she herself condemned. "I will. Are there those whom I should be aware of now?"

"You are the very best at what you do, my darling." He gave her a small smile.

"You mean to say," she whispered, "that you have no proof yet of those whom you suspect?"

"You read my mind well. Even after all this time apart."

His voice vibrated through her body and the intoxicating effect made her wonder if in all these years he had taken lovers. Whoever they had been—for with his looks, he had surely had them—she was shockingly, maddeningly jealous. "Do I? How can I possibly when I do not even know the name of the man I address?"

His real name, she knew. But his code name?

He gave her a small bow. "You address *Monsieur Noir.*"

She grinned. "Apt for a man few know well."

"You, *ma tigresse*, have known me best."

And you me. For who else have you and I ever trusted, but each other? "Be quick about your return, will you? I yearn for good company."

"Do you? Poor darling." He brushed his index finger along her cheek and raised her chin so that he could whisper against her skin. "There is so much to say, Solange, *ma chère comtesse.*"

"I promise to be as swift as circumstances permit."

She scowled at him. "Oh, I would so hate to rush you."

"Sarcasm, my beauty, does not become you. Have patience. God knows, where you are concerned, I suddenly lack any." He wrapped her close, his massive arms the safe haven they had always been when she was eight and fifteen. Now that she was thirty, he pressed her to his body and this time, as no other, he put his mouth upon her own and kissed her like the phantom who had possessed her imagination for all the lonely intervening years. He caressed her lips, a tender mating. On a curse she knew connoted his sensual delight in her, he steadied her to her feet. With a tap to her nose and wicked wink of his eye, he turned and strode away.

She watched him go. Touched her fingers to the swell of her lips. And understood with his kiss, he made a new promise to her. One conveying more than rescue. More than comfort. More than camaraderie.

Monsieur Noir. You tell me tales with your lips meant for love between my exquisite sheets.

She stomped her foot, impatience one of her few flaws.

How many days and nights until I see you again, you tormenting man?

Chapter Two

October 4, 1815

Solange sorted the bank notes she had ac-
quired as her winnings at whist tonight at Lady
Whimplemore's palazzo. Four hundred and
twenty pounds. Not a bad reward for enduring a
most boring evening.

Another one without any word from *Monsieur Noir.*

Where the hell was he? Four days now and
not a sign. Not a peep. Not a note. And definitely
no appearances in anyone's garden.

Yet he had appeared in her daydreams and
her nightly ones, as well. All–all!–wearing that
deftly tailored black mask. Oh, bother him!

She should go to bed, forget his lax behavior
in the elixir of sleep.

Ba! If she could find it.

She shot from her chair, dropping her merino
wool dressing gown to the *chaise longue* and
heading for her huge mahogany bed upon the

gilded platform. Her cousin, James, had gleefully informed her that the gigantic bed had been carved for some licentious Renaissance duke and his mistresses. All three of them in it at the same time with him. Blast them for their ingenuity.

Meanwhile, she was here alone and the night was cold. The spring air chilling her, making her nipples bud and her skin prickle. She stopped short at the dais, awareness that her body's reactions were not to the weather but to the man she wanted. Wanted and did not have.

Her hands closed over her naked breasts. Wanton fantasies of *Noir* kissing her again wafted through her mind. She wanted his lips on her ear, her throat, her nipples. Her—. No! She cursed.

Oh, why should she think of him this way? He was the savior of her young life. A ghost, a genie. Here, there, then not at all. So appropriately named *Noir*. Black. Void. For what did she know of him? Nothing about the past fifteen years of his life. Everything about his parents, his home, his older brother, his unparalleled courage in the face of men demanding his death. Why should she care about him? Where he was, how he fared. *Because he is one of the few people*

*on this earth who ever deeply cared about you—
and took great pains to demonstrate it.*

Closing her eyes, she remembered once more the warmth of his body against hers in the garden. Why did he obsess her? She had known him twice briefly as a child, now once for minutes standing in a maze. Why should she want him with her? For more than comfort.

Ahhh! She whirled for her bed. Big, broad and empty. Oh, hell. Would she have no peace? If only he would make haste, do his duty as her contact and as replacement for *Monsieur de la Guerre.*

A light knock came to the outer door of her suite.

"Solange, dearest," her cousin's wife, Maryanne, called to her from the hall. "Have you retired? If not, do let me in as I have something for you! I know you love surprises and this is a beautiful one."

Sitting up, Solange sprang for her robe, then rushed for the door and flung it wide. "Is it? I am always greedy for new delights no matter the hour. What do you have?" *From whom?*

"A package!" Maryanne held up a box wrapped in white satin tied up with a gigantic pink bow. Her blue eyes danced as she handed it over. "Scrumptious looking, I do say, my girl, and I am absolutely feral to see what's inside."

Solange chuckled at her cousin's wife, a cheerful lass from Edinburgh, whose brogue and fiery looks matched her unpredictable personality. "Who brought it?"

"Very mysterious. The butler does not know. He responded to the bell and a ragamuffin thrust it into his hand. I asked him for more details, I did. To no avail. But such lovely stuff does not need an introduction, would you think?"

"No. But then I wonder what the occasion might be." Solange took the box, rattled it, heard nothing and proceeded to her little reading table to open it. "It's not my birthday."

Maryanne strode right behind her. "Perhaps, a new admirer?"

"An intriguing idea," she led Maryanne on, wishing this were from *Noir*, but wondering if that *roué*, Prince Giorgio were attempting to buy her affections with presents she could not refuse. "But who?"

"Prince Giorgio?"

"I'm to see him tomorrow." *God help me.* "He shows me his new silk factory."

"No matter, dearest. Any new suitor is thrilling. And you have so many that I wonder you haven't yet chosen one of them to marry!"

Putting the package down, Solange stroked the fat pink ribbon and smiled. "I have no need of a husband."

"You never know you need one until you find the one you cannot live without. Now open this! Do!"

Solange pulled at the end of the ribbon, then lifted the top. Inside, a frothy garment shimmered in the candlelight.

"Oh! My!" Maryanne was agog.

Solange herself commented on the exquisite nature of the fabric. She touched a fingertip to the gossamer-thin cotton and saw at once, it was a chemise of purest white.

She lifted it out, a reverence in her motions. The translucence sparkled as she held it aloft. And a folded card of vellum floated to the floor.

"A love note!" Maryanne cooed like a girl over her first beau. "How thrilling!"

Solange stared at it as it lay upon the carpet. She bent to pick it up, her heart in her throat as she flipped it open to read one word. 'Tonight.'

Tonight? Where? At what time?

"I will leave you to enjoy it!" Maryanne waggled her fingers at her as she padded toward the far door, leaving Solange to stare after her. "I daresay from the looks of that garment, that missive had better be a love note."

"Why, Maryanne," Solange chided her as she clutched the paper to her chest and let her eyes dance merrily at her cousin, "it comes from my banker."

"Ah, yes, of course it does. All bankers think only of scandalous underclothes. Is he calling in a loan? Or making a deposit on his own investment of time and courtship? No, no. Do not tell me. I am returning to my husband. Enjoy yourself." She winked. "Good night."

Solange drifted in the strong waves of a deep and satisfying moment. She rocked and swayed upon the sea, and though the wind blew with howling ferocity and the water churned, she was quite safe. Cocooned against a marvelously warm chest. Bound by corded arms. Secured by one long wool-clad male leg to a sculpted body. One she knew and yet one strangely startling to her in its well-hewn proportions.

Agile fingers stroked her hair, warm breaths tickled her earlobe, demanding lips trailed along her throat. And she undulated in his arms to glance at a vision so black, she knew her captor to be the man who as a youth had freed her from all dark despairs. *"Noir,"* she whispered his newest name and sank back into his embrace, content and secure in the knowledge this was no dream. "I waited for you. Not knowing where or when."

"My apologies, *ma douce.*" He nestled her nearer to him, their body heat mingling beneath the wealth of blankets. "I came as soon as I could."

"You climbed to the balcony?"

"But of course. I relied upon you remembering my talents at scaling walls."

"And swimming lakes? Jumping from haystacks? I could not forget." Hugging him, she pressed her face to his throat. His linen shirt lay open there and she could easily inhale his soothing musk. The lemon and sandalwood mingled with the more primal scent she remembered from their first and second encounters. "I am so pleased you are here. Your note tells me nothing."

"I know." He chuckled and ran his fingers through her riot of curls to fan the strands upon the pillows. In this same manner had he soothed her when she was eight and then again at fifteen. "I wanted to come. I wanted this. You in my arms again. I never forgot what we were for each other."

She was tired enough, languid and secure enough to be as revealing. "Nor I. The world is very cold, and when you have known one who has saved you from its bitterness, you remember him always."

"And I, you." Through the sheer chemise she had donned on impulse, he stroked her back. His tenderness recalled the relaxing touch he'd often used in those weeks as they had escaped the nightmare that was the Paris mobs and ran toward Normandy and freedom.

"Ah, no. I did so very little to secure our deliverance."

"The time you gave the diversion to the blacksmith while I stole his only horse?"

"Poor bugger," she said and the two of them chuckled sadly.

"When Bonaparte is finally gone, you and I shall return and pay that man for the horse."

Solange tipped up her head to look into his eyes. But in the dead of night with the drapes closed and no candles lit, she could see only the barest outlines of his classic features. "Do you think he might still be alive?"

"We could pray so."

"I do. I often have done. I am thrilled you wish to pay him. A fine idea."

"There is also the smuggler in Calais who must be due some recompense."

She laughed. "That wretch! He was so furious when he found us in the galley larder he wanted to throw us overboard. What money should we give him?"

"Equivalent to passage across the Channel, *ma cherie*. It's only fair."

"So true." She snuggled back into his arms and marveled that they felt so dear, so natural after such a long absence. "Without his forbearance, I would not have landed in England to find my Aunt Minette. Nor would I be here with my cousin now."

"We owe so many a debt of gratitude. I wonder if we can repay them all." His voice grew gruff with melancholy.

"Do we not show our gratitude by what we now do?" she asked him, her own somber brown study coming upon her in a thick wave of gloom.

"Aye, we do," he murmured and placed his lips upon her forehead. "We each pay our prices. Your *Monsieur de la Guerre* paid the highest. He was my runner."

After their meeting in the garden, she'd concluded that *Noir* had been *de la Guerre's master*. Their network rules demanded few know identities save those necessary. She searched *Noir*'s face for confirmation of that. Again, she saw little in the cloak of night.

"Solange, he was one of my three runners. I assigned him to you more than two years ago."

"To me? You did this?" Given how bold she knew him to be, she should not be surprised at this revelation. Still, it stung that *Noir* had known where she was, how she was and she had known nothing of him. "You have been doing this that long?"

"Eight years. Perhaps longer. Time seems immaterial."

"Etienne!"

At the use of his given name, he inhaled. "*Oui, ma cherie*. I have been your coordinator these past two years. I know what you have accomplished and I am struck by your successes—and by your bravery." He brushed her hair from her ear, and were the night not so dark, she was certain she might have seen him gazing into her eyes with reverence. "You have caught so many agents for us, I am in awe."

Humility was her touchstone. Honesty her asset. "I use those tools God gave me."

He barked in laughter. "Charm and beauty. Enticing every male over ten in breeches. And yet none has found his way to your bed."

That Etienne knew this was a testament to his skills at espionage. Still, she bristled that her life should be an open page for him. While he had become a cipher to her. "I do not wish to earn my ribbons by prostituting myself."

"Laudable. I have watched you for years. Even before I recommended you for work with the Home Department, I remembered your expert skill with a pistol and dagger."

She tsked. "I only frightened my opponents. Whereas you?" She let that thought drift. "You got me into this." She teased to show her pleasure at his vigilance over her life. "Why do that, eh?"

"I know you best. Your despair of tyrants of all stripes. So too did I know how you endured your marriage to a silly, vacuous man. No wonder that your marriage was loveless. No surprise that you needed direction, purpose."

She ran her hand through his satin hair. The sensation heated her blood and she pressed her thighs together. "You taught me that fear can be a tool to defeat your opponents. You are excellent at your trade, *Monsieur Noir*."

He touched the tip of her nose. "The very best, *Princesse de Nevers*."

She shivered at the mention of the title which had been hers as princess of the blood of the Bourbons. But the Revolution had outstripped its principles and Bonaparte had usurped them for his own ends. "Let us not speak of the past. Stroke my back as you did so long ago. Only that calms me."

"I remember." His careful fingers brushed along her ribcage and over the chemise he had sent her with his note. "You wore my gift."

She trembled at his husky words, undulating toward him and knowing full well that below her waist she was scandalously naked. "Mmm. I am a glutton for lingerie. I venture you knew this, too, else you would not have bought it."

"A convenient excuse to send you a gift," he murmured, his hand now cupping her bare hip.

She tried to still her racing heart. How often had she dreamed of having him touch her like this? Since she had been a bride, forced into wedlock with a boring fop. Since she had heard other women whisper about worthy lovers who excited them. She never knew any other men bold enough to merit imagining them in her bed. None as handsome. None as chivalrous. None as daring as he had been at fourteen, or at twenty-one or now at the ripe old age of thirty-six. He had rescued her over and over. How many other men had ever saved her? No one from the mob. No one from Napoleon. No one from crashing boredom.

Mon Dieu. She had never wanted any other man. In her dreams. In her arms. She yearned only for him, then and now. Yet she must be prudent. "Tell me quickly what my task is."

His nails stroked patterns on her upper thigh. "Your cousin has three aides, two of whom I suspect of treason," he told her, his voice oddly gruff. "One of them must be passing word to Murat's Italian armies about the British navy here, but I am not certain which one."

"Armand Arcineaux?"

"Armand, our little duke from the Gironde? Perhaps."

"I like him for it best," she revealed as she pressed a lavish kiss to *Noir's* strong throat. "He is so forward."

"Yes, quite," *Noir* murmured, his palm lifting her thigh and hooking it over his own. Opening her to him, luring her onward to a sultry union with him. "Has he approached you? Attempted to seduce you?"

"Often." She swallowed hard, her sensitive flesh afire, her core swelling with ferocious interest.

"I think I shall kill him." He skimmed his hot hand up the crease of her inner thigh.

"Not until we determine his guilt." She tipped up her hips, her moist folds flush against his warm fingers. "How warm you are, my sweet *Noir*."

"Darling, we must not." His body froze.

She rubbed her skin against his gentle fingertips. "Why? Have you an appointment?"

"Solange," he chastised her, but buried his lips in the valley of her breasts. "You are delicious."

She held him there, joyous that she could attract him and hold him in such thrall. Once more, she pushed her tender flesh against his hand.

"Listen to me, *ma belle*." He raised his face. Though she could not see him, she knew he frowned, attempting to be stern. "We know the

Italians have learned of our fleet here in port and off Capri. And—"

"I hear you," she whispered, pressing against his hips to cradle that rigid part of him which would satisfy her most.

"Darling, no," he objected and pulled away.

"Yes, oh, yes," she told him and knew on a stroke of brilliance that this was the answer to her longings for a magnificent man in her arms. She had not taken any lovers because only one— this one—would ever do. Her hand skimmed along his waist, his hip, his leg clad in tight breeches, his flies bulging with his obvious interest in her.

He caught her hand, stilled it. "I am telling you about our spy."

"I know you are, my adorable man, and you may indeed continue." She flung away the covers, pushing him to his back. Against her ivory sheets, his face and his form became living, breathing man. No mirage made of fragments from her past. No fantasy made of hope, but a lover. She worked at his flies, popping his buttons.

Suddenly he was helping her, pushing down the wool, grabbing her by the waist and lifting her so that he could capture one aching nipple,

chemise and all, lick it, suck it, feast on it. She cried out as he left one breast and seized the other. *Dieu*, she had never known such possession.

She straddled him, one hand to his hip, the other gripping his impressive cock. "Oh, darling! This is how well you want me? Why could you not come to tell me before this?"

He muttered nonsense about bad timing and poor circumstances. Then he skimmed his hand along her ribs, lifted the chemise and stripped it over her head. His palms cupped her breasts, their wealth spilling over his long fingers as he led her toward him. He captured one bare nipple, groaning his pleasure, while she hung over him, enchanted as he took the other nipple and honored it with his kisses and his little nips. Shifting, he traced the outline of nether lips and stroked her core with deft forays inside her. "I will do better than to tell you, my pretty."

He rolled her to the mattress. Yanking off his own shirt, he loomed above her, beautifully naked. Though she could curse the lack of light, she discovered him now with her fingers and her mouth. His clavicle was wide, the hollow deep. His ribs harshly etched with muscle. His stomach trim, the arrow line of hair to his groin, thin and furry. His waist was deeply indented, his hips flaring enough to imply he would be a powerful lover. His thatch of hair was thick, his balls huge and warm with potential. His shaft, the most impressive element of all, was long as her hand and thick. And when she caressed him, his cock flexed as he growled with delight.

Grabbing her hands above her head, he pinned her to the bed. "You are aggressive."

"My best quality and to your benefit," she told him in a rush as she settled beneath him, her thighs falling open in invitation.

He uttered a profanity in French and spread her legs even wider. His fingers darting to her intimate flesh, he parted her folds and bent to blow cool air against her flaming flesh. She mewled and he inserted two fingers inside her to stroke her until she cried out for more of him.

"So damn wet. Such a sweet must be savored."

"Do," she urged him on a husky whisper.

Chuckling, he sank over her and kissed her from the top of her seam to the bottom. His tongue laved her, then darted deep inside.

Her mouth open, her mind gone, she plucked at his arms and demanded more, more and quickly, too!

In one swift pull, he had her legs up on his thighs so that he impaled her on his stunningly massive cock. The world went still. Silent. With only a growing compulsion inside her burning body to have him make love to her at long last.

"Ah, *mon Dieu*." He pulled out of her, leaving her to bat at his chest. "No. No! We know nothing of tomorrow. I will not risk it with consequences."

A child? "I doubt I—"

"No, Solange. We will not argue on this. I should not have come to your bed. A mistake." He cursed beneath his breath.

Her body empty and pulsing, she caught back a sob of regret and outrage. She never begged a man or anyone for anything. Never. But here, now, she willed herself to total stillness as he left her alone in her bed. She stared silently at him as he pulled on his clothes and, shoes in hand, padded to her balcony doors.

"*Adieu*, Solange. Find me our informant."

"And when I do?" she asked, coldly realistic about her duty and her prospects for changing

Noir's mind in one evening's mindless and inter-rupted passion.

"I shall find you."

"Well, then." As a beguiling woman who un-derstood men, seduction and secrets, she reverted to a ploy she knew would rebuke and entice. "*Adieu, mon ami.*"

In the light from the moon, he faced her and at her words, he scowled.

Je suis désolé, Noir.

Never were you merely my friend. But now, you are so much more.

Chapter Three

October 5, 1815

Solange posed this way and that in front of her gilded cheval glass, dressed only in thigh-high white stockings and her newest gift. The chemise trimmed in hand-worked lace from Venice's Burano Island was a treasure that skimmed over her full breasts. Her large nipples formed shadows beneath the gauzy fabric. She put her hands on the swell of her hips, turning this way and that, and wondered if *Noir* would ever see her in this fabulous garment.

This second chemise *Noir* had sent her had arrived this morning, wrapped in the same luscious trapping of white and pink with a note of black script with two words. "Your Prince." He implied, she knew, a misdirection, for though the message came from *Noir*, he was no prince. Indeed, the words were an indication that her journey out to the road to Rome with Giorgio was a trip useful to *Noir*. Whatever he had learned since last night's visit here had pointed to the nefarious doings of the hawk-like Italian. It was her job to learn more about the man and give the information to *Noir*.

In the meantime, she sighed that *Noir* was not here to share the sight of her supple body in the exquisite garment. She would plan to show him and delight both of them with it as soon as possible. Tonight, she dared to hope. *Irritating man.*

Her English maid, a thin little blonde, whom she had brought with her from London, stood behind her smiling, her arms full of Solange's bombazine day dress. "That is a nice bit, milady. The gentleman knows how to please. A shame to cover it! Shall we continue?"

"Yes, of course, Cora." Solange allowed the servant to dress her, snapping the tabs and arranging the exquisite folds. The forest green fabric with organza ribbons at the bodice was a bright spring piece that complemented her flawless skin and rosy cheeks. As Cora secured the laces at her back, Solange fluffed up the bodice with its delicate edges of the Venetian lace to peek over the organza. The effect was to frame her breasts beautifully for the carriage ride. "Only enough to tease."

"He is a hungry man, Lady Starling," Cora concluded. "Tom told it about downstairs that Prince Giorgio once even attempted to seduce Lady Moreland."

"Tom? The footman said this about the Prince and Maryanne...Lady Moreland?" Her cousin's wife was pure as snow. And if the man had accosted her, Maryanne would have told her husband. And Tom the footman was bold to carry such a tale. For idle gossip in the house, Tom could lose his position. She wondered if James knew of Tom's prospensity to wag his tongue.

"Yes, ma'am. The prince tried it here in the embassy, too."

Solange frowned. "What else do they say downstairs about him?"

"He's a roo." Cora continued her work, tugging at Solange's gown.

"A roo? Ah. *Oui*. You mean a *roué*! That one can see at first glance."

"But not rich. Or Tom says so."

Was this the idle chatter of servants? "How can our footman know this?"

"The prince's coachman loves our scotch," Cora offered as her green eyes twinkled. "And when he's in his cups, Tom says he's got loose lips. The other night during the Mask, the coachman sat down in our kitchen and told us all that the prince is in debt."

Is that so? "And did the coachman leave us with any ideas as to whom our prince may owe his fortunes?"

"Count Borofsky."

"The Russian ambassador?" An ally of the British and therefore, not necessarily a questionable acquaintance for Giorgio.

"Yes, ma'am." Cora primped and fussed with the drape of Solange's bombazine skirts. "And the mayor of Naples."

Well now. That fat little weasel would rob his blind mother of her last penny. But of what use this was, Solange could not venture. She would store it for reference. "*Merci*, Cora. Let me know if you learn more about any of them, *oui*?"

The maid nodded, then handed Solange her muff. "I'd say you take the cherry wool today, milady. The spring air is cool and you are in the open air for hours."

"A wise suggestion. Meanwhile, you'll be in need of a coat, riding up on the box. Do get that and we'll go."

Solange waited while her maid hurried to her little sleeping room to pick up her own service- able cloak. She pulled on her gloves, smiled at Cora as she returned and then led them both down the stairs. Silently, the two women pad- ded down the carpeted marble steps that wound round and round. As they did, Solange noticed in the drawing room to the left, two men stood talking. She saw only their lower torsos and legs. One was Giorgio, dressed in his tailored black superfine trousers. The other was a ser- vant of the household, for his shoes of dull black leather were the ones the entire male staff wore. His livery with the red strip down the side of his breeches confirmed he belonged to the British embassy. But one thing which did not denote his status as a servant was the way his hands clenched and pointed in anger as he con- versed. One hand, his left, bore a large tattoo, a burned mark resembling a black eagle. This was the mark of one who at one time had been im- prisoned by Napoleon. More odd was the fact that this servant spoke Italian. Easily, it seemed. What member of their English staff spoke Italian smartly enough to talk with Prince Giorgio? She knew of none.

Solange picked up her pace. To catch him, glimpse him was her goal.

Cora could scare keep up. "My lady? You'll trip!"

The sound of the maid's words stopped the men's conversation. Abruptly, the servant stepped away from Giorgio so that Solange came upon the Italian walking out to the grand staircase to meet her.

"Good day to you, *Signora* Starling." He bowed.

Should she ask him who he'd been talking with?

No. She'd learn who it was in other ways.

"Good afternoon," she bid him.

The prince sought her hand to kiss. His lips were, as ever, repulsively oh so cold and wet. "I cannot express how delighted I am to escort you to view my beautiful silks."

She extracted her hand and smiled at him, self-satisfied ogre. "I am prepared to swoon." *Over them, oui. You? We shall see how much you can amuse me.*

"I shall endeavor to ensure you enjoy every moment."

Only if you reveal new facets of your personality, dear prince.

But hours later, sitting in his closed brougham without benefit of hot bricks to warm her cold feet, and her arms sore from pushing back his incessant advances, Solange had learned very little new about the man, his debts or his friends. She could only count the minutes until she returned to James's residence, her suite, hot tea and an opportunity to find the servant on the staff whose left hand bore the burned black eagle mark of a former prisoner of Napoleon. Why would a servant in James's employ have an argument with an Italian prince? The two should never speak, save for curt pleasantries. What could be the connection between them?

"Have you known my cousin James since he become the ambassador here?" she asked as she tried a new tact to amuse the Prince and dissuade him from his seduction of her.

"*Si*, my Solanj-a. We met many years ago in Roma. I was the consul there from my king's court."

The king to whom he referred was the one who had returned to rule here after Murat fled in late May. "James was the aide to the English ambassador then."

"He was. We have been friends ever since." Giorgio took her gloved hand in his.

"I see." She permitted him to paw her hand as if she were a puppy. "I suppose then...you have helped each other with many things?"

"*Si, si,* we have. I have helped him learn Italian and find a good boot maker." They laughed. "Also, to find a house to please his wife."

"Oh, yes. Maryanne is very exacting about her accommodations. Her furniture and her staff." *How do you know that servant you spoke with today?*

"I like your cousin. But he does not bend to our ways."

"No? How so?"

"He does not like our practice of gifts."

"Gifts?"

"*Si.* Take the mayor for example."

"The mayor." *Very well. Let us talk of him. Corrupt little man that he is.*

"*Si.* That man is always in office. No matter who rules. And as he survives, he is always with his hand out."

"This is true? He takes bribes?" She feigned false shock.

Giorgio chuckled. "A man from Napoli is nothing unless his palm is greased."

"Wonderful." She remembered the shriveled creature from Nevers who used to come and try to squeeze coins from her father to run the town granary at a more favorable price to the peasants. "Will that ever change?"

"I doubt it. For some, it is the only way to survive."

"Bribery. Did Murat bribe officials here?"

"Naturally!" Giorgio flourished a hand. "Every one does."

"Does James?"

Giorgio's eyebrows knit together. "You think this of your cousin?"

"I don't know." *Dangerous territory here.* "Should I?"

"Ask him. That is, if you wish to truly know. And...why would you?"

"Just trying to learn how things work here in Napoli." She beamed at him, innocence oozing from her.

The coach fell silent.

He toyed with her fingers.

She permitted it at a loss how to proceed and not spoil her act.

"I hope this afternoon has proven enjoyable for you, *bella*," Giorgio told her as he settled to her dismay on the squabs beside her. "I have heard of your habit, Solanj-a, of spending your sizable winnings at whist on lingerie. Venetian. Damascene. Expensive. Lacy, frilly, decidedly decadent lingerie."

"I cannot imagine who told you this about my winnings," she replied feigning coy enjoyment of his revelation, knowing she must draw him out on personal matters or lose her chance today. "If it was my maid Cora, up there on the box with your driver, I shall be most decidedly unhappy with her."

"Does it matter how I learned?" he asked with a wicked eye on the bolts of cloth in the seat across from them. His gifts were many. Her hopes were dwindling. How could she escape his lechery? "Only that you are happy matters to me. That is why I brought these along."

She looked him in the eye with a paramour's enticement. Could she fake her surprise at his attempt to buy her favors? "You cannot mean they are–?"

"For you? But of course." He inched closer, his hip and thigh pressing into hers, his arm coming round her shoulders, his hand cupping her face. "You know what I wish."

"I'm at a loss, Your Highness." She averted her head, avoiding his lips.

"No, *bella*, no. You are a wise woman. A widow. A prize." His hand dropped to the collar of her coat, working at the clasp and opening it to drop inside and toy with her ribbons and the lace at her bodice. "I must have an evening with you."

"Really, Giorgio!" She squirmed beneath his insistent hand that found her breast and squeezed so hard she yelped and leaned away. "You mistake my friendly nature for—"

"You are a woman who needs a man in her bed. I am that man. I have shown you." He slid along the seat to haul her into his embrace. His chilly lips descended to her throat and her heaving bosom.

"This is hardly my bed, sir!" She shrank to the side of the coach. "And the gift of a few bolts of silk cannot buy my affections."

"I can give you more." He pawed at her bombazine bodice, making her gasp at his effrontery. "What would you have, aside from me inside this lovely body?"

To learn your secrets? "I would wish to learn everything about you. How to please you. Thrill you." *Merde!* Was she insane? But how else was she to learn his habits, his friends, his contacts with James's staff?

"Ah, my dream—"

She pushed at his chest. "But I am a lady, dear man, and I need a respectable courtship."

That stopped him in the midst of his mauling. He caught her chin and stared down into her eyes. "To be my permanent lover? You would commit to this?"

"I would." She straightened her spine and brushed at her skirts. "But you must give me my due, Your Highness. You must court me as the lady I am."

He arched a brow, his ribald nature supplanted in a flash by a startling and contrasting demeanor as a bird of prey. "Like the *princessa* you are by birth? Is that what you demand?"

"*Absolutement!*" she deferred to her native tongue. "I am a woman of breeding and refinement. And you, sir? You are not married and you may take a wife. If you wish me in your bed, then you must acquire me in the time-honored manner."

"Court you like a love-sick boy?" he asked, astonishment in his voice and face.

She waved a hand. "No less."

"You are demanding."

"But for your patience, you shall have a just reward." *As I shall have mine.*

"I shall take you until you scream with delight," he cooed with a grin and grabbed her hand to put it to his groin. His cock, she could detect, was long and hard but skinny as her hair brush. And his balls seemed...ah, yes...miniscule. Did his resolution match the size of his tiny testicles? She had to learn. She would. And if her deception were the best way to find the traitor within her cousin's household, she would go as far as she must. Even if...dear lord...she must climb into bed with this creature.

She reclaimed her hand and peered at him with jaundiced eye. "And I, dear Giorgio, will unman you with my charms."

"Ah, my succulent Solanj-a." He kissed her fingertips and then his own. "I await the day."

Here's hoping I may get you to rue it.

Rushing across the portico to the front door of the embassy, Solange was a flutter to escape Giorgio's salacious grasp. Her invitation to court her and marry her had momentarily suppressed his ravenous appetite, but she felt violated. Compromised. In deed and principle. She needed to breathe cleaner air. Far away from him.

What have you done, Solange? She panicked as the butler opened the front door.

"My lady," Quinn said, blinking, "you are home early."

"I am. Thank you," she told him as she turned to shrug out of her coat. As she scampered up the staircase to her suite, Cora followed her and called after her. Once inside the sanctity of her own rooms, Solange reviewed the implications of what she had pledged to Giorgio.

"Madam?" Cora asked, alarm in her wide eyes as she gazed at Solange's frantic pacing. "What is wrong? Can I get you a brandy? Draw you a bath?"

A glimpse of the thin English maid who shivered in her own sodden cloak brought Solange back to her senses. "Never worry about me. You go have a warm bath and a change of clothes."

"But ma'am, you need that before me."

"Order hot water for me after you return." She headed for the stairs and a task she knew

she must accomplish. But meeting Giorgio had been her priority. "I'll return in minutes."

"Where are you going?"

"Where I should have gone before," Solange muttered to herself as she scurried down the marble stairs to the first floor and then round to the back hall and down one more flight of wooden stairs. To the servants quarters.

Chapter Four

Evening, October 5, 1815

The evening seemed eternal! She read Byron and fretted. Sent two hot bricks up to Cora, brought low by the rain today to her bed in the upstairs servants quarters. Then Solange wrote to her Aunt Minette, James's mother, and paced the floor. She even played a vicious and solitary game of chess and threw the board, pieces and all, across the room. Still, *Noir* did not come.

If she could not relieve herself from the anxiety of holding her secrets, she would look like the ravages of hell at breakfast. Why did he not appear? Her visit below stairs had been most profitable. Her visit with James, minutes later in his study, much more so. *Noir* must learn it all.

Yet, what detained him? *Where are you, Etienne? Are you reluctant to come tonight? Afraid I might not welcome you? Or need you?*

Clutching her dressing gown around her, she marched to her boudoir window three stories above the Via Espana. No one walked out at this small hour of the morning. The rain broke into torrents, lightning crashed and a downpour obscured the details of the other houses along the boulevard.

A sleek black coach trotted past her door, only to pause at the garden. Did a figure emerge from the cab? She wiped the moisture from the glass, but her vision became no clearer. Her hands upon the latch, she satisfied herself that her balcony doors were indeed unlocked and accessible from the garden terrace.

Climbing into her bed wearing one thin nightdress, she lay on her back, folded her hands like a day-old corpse and waited for *Noir*.

She heard the latch on the French doors give and the pounding of the deluge become louder as someone entered from the balcony and shut out the sounds of the world. Exhausted but satisfied he had at last arrived, Solange called to him from the bed.

In the flashes of lightning, she watched his powerful silhouette stop and scan the room.

"Do not stand there and drip on my carpet, *mon cher.*" She flung back her covers. "The night is ugly and we both need warmth."

"Solange, no," he murmured, pleading with her for reprieve from the intimacy she offered.

"Come, *Noir.* I will not leave this bed."

Cursing, he divested himself of cloak, boots, coat and stock. He left them draped over a wooden bench near the doors. Striding to her side, he slid in beside her. Once this close, she knew he would do as he had always done when this near to her. He encompassed her in his arms and she lifted her bare leg to curl around his hips and welcome him to her. He did not object, neither did he move.

"You are chilled," she murmured, a frisson of delight traveling her spine as she embraced him.

"I am never ill."

"How well I recall. You could eat nothing, hunt for game or scout for soldiers all day and never tire."

"To weaken is to lose," he told her, his lips to her forehead, his tone grim. "You went out with him today."

"I did," she offered simply, replaying the tone of *Noir's* voice, listening for the jealousy she sought like a starving child.

"What did you learn?"

Her palm upon his chest, she caressed his well-hewn muscles beneath his waistcoat and his shirt. Then with an indifference she used like a knife, she said, "He wishes to have me as his own."

Noir snorted. "Bastard. Of course he wants the lovely English woman. So does every man worth his salt in this city."

Wondering if *Noir* would admit to counting himself among those men, she snuggled into him and kissed his throat.

He cupped her nape, holding her still. "You refused him?"

She sighed. "You and I both suspect him of treachery. We have tried to learn his actions and failed. It seems the best course to draw closer to him. I concluded I should accept him."

Noir pulled back, their gazes locked as the lightning struck to illuminate the room. "You do not wish the man."

"I wish only to complete my mission."

Noir's arms tightened around her. "Such sacrifice is not required."

"Of course it is. You know it. Recount what you have lost since the Terror. Your entire family. Your lands and your—"

"I did not relinquish those. They were taken from me."

"And what do you sacrifice to gain any of it back?"

"Do I work for that?" he asked as if he had never before considered it.

"You live in the shadows," she persisted. "Running spies in foreign cities. How do you live? Where? Why have I not seen you—" she tempered her tones of sorrow, "—not seen you in years?" She pressed a tiny kiss to the corner of his mouth.

He flinched. "You have no idea what I have given to the cause of restoration of my rights."

She heard the bitterness in his words. "I can imagine, *mon cher*. I can help you and you must not forbid it."

"Not to give your body to a man who will not respect you! No!"

She yanked from his grasp and rolled to her feet. Naked, she rejoiced when the storm obliged her with another bright strike of lightning. *Noir* drank her in, his gaze running over her naked body as if he imbibed wine for his soul. "You cannot stop me, Etienne."

"Darling Solange, he is not worthy to touch you." He sprang from the bed and came round

to press her to the wall. "How can you expect me to sanction such an act?"

"We must learn who aids Murat in this house. Time grows short. If Murat invades and wins back Naples, Bonaparte can return to the Continent!"

"To hell with Bonaparte!" He took her by the shoulders. "The British sail him off to St. Helena."

"No matter. He escaped them six months ago. He could again!"

"Never!" *Noir* gave her a shake. "I will not let you take that Italian crow to your bed!"

"You have no say!" she incited him.

"I do! I have earned a say. Once, twice and now..."

"Now, what?" She wrenched to be free of him.

"After last night?"

"We shared nothing!" she flung at him. *You saw to it.*

"We could not!"

"No? You left me wanting, needing—" She pushed at him. "After all we are to each other and all these years of yearning, you left me empty and wanting you, Etienne."

He yanked her to him. "How could I make love to you?"

"How could you not?" she demanded.

"I cannot have you!"

"Who forbids it?"

"My conscience! What if we loved and tomorrow escapes us?"

"*Mon cher*," she mourned, "it always did."

He stared at her, hunger and remorse in his stance and in his eyes, desire. "Why do you think I never came to you before this? Why do you think I ran a courier between us? Why?"

She raised her chin and arched her brows at him.

"I did not want to see you. As you grew older, after you were widowed, I knew your life and I knew if we met again what would happen between us."

"Did you? Sure of your charms, are you?" she taunted him, roiled he had purposely stayed away from her and yet proud—triumphant—that he had longed for her.

He pulled her flush against him, the proof of his desire a hard brand against her belly. "No coyness for me, *ma petite*. You and I came to care for each other long ago. When survival depended on trust and mutual responsibility."

"Still you deny us both any pleasure." She wrapped her arms around his waist and cuddled so near she could be absorbed into his skin. "The finest bliss I ever knew was with you. The exhilaration of escape. The thrill of victory against all those hundreds who hunted us. The years between our meetings have been so fraught with the perils of ordinary living. And no affection. Or love. How can you refuse the opportunity to seize bliss?"

His expression, so bleak, so stern, shattered.

"The devil knows. I do not." He caught her mouth with his and ravished her with his kiss. He was starved, savage. His lips on her own, she opened her mouth to him, his tongue and his claim. She had pushed him to this. Knowing finally in these past days that only he could be her match. Only he, her mate. She had yearned for this carnal union, but she wanted more from him. His jealousy was a beginning. His edict against bedding the Italian a finer satisfaction. Tonight, she would have all he had to give her. She undulated against him, her lips, her arms, her legs open to him.

He put his hands to her waist, his gaze possessive, primal.

She quivered.

But her anticipation was so short, so brief.

He seized her against him, arched her up, his arm around her waist, and bent to suck her breast into his ravenous mouth. His tongue laved her, while his other hand cupped her other breast and rolled her nipple between two fingers. "How many nights I watched you with George Starling. Going to Drury Lane. To dinner parties and weddings. Dancing at balls. I had saved you. I had saved you from death, not once but twice—and that old man had the right to take you as his own? Absurd!"

Solange swooned at his declaration, her hands skimming the sculpted power of his back and the taut swell of his buttocks. "Etienne, George is gone, my darling. I want only you."

He sank to his knees, his hands drifting over her curves until he held her at the thighs. He kissed the froth of hair at their juncture. Then he pushed her legs open. "I have dreamed of this and you. I have imagined how you smell, how you taste." He sank a finger along her seam. "Wet and warm. Open here for me. I will have you completely now at last."

She spread her thighs, her balance a precarious thing in her haste.

He growled in approval and probed his tongue inside her.

She lost her breath. His devotion and his talent taking her mind as well. He nuzzled further inside her, cursing and then tugging her to the floor. She lay beneath him, her legs bent at the knees, her arms circling him as he undid his flies and thrust his breeches down his hips. "Hurry, hurry, I am so—"

"Filled." He slipped inside her, driving to the hilt, and she vibrated with the enchantment to the roots of her hair and the tips of her fingers. She gasped in an ecstasy that George had never granted her. *Noir* rocked inside her turbulent, wild, his cock a wondrous appendage. Unlike last night, he slammed into her with a rhythm, a thrust and devotion that shocked her for its force. She plucked at his arms, crazed to feel him closer. But he pulled out, eliciting a cry from her.

"No! You will not go!" She caught his wrists, near to hysteria that he would leave her again.

"I do not go," he whispered, cupping her face, his thumbs brushing her cheeks. "I come closer." To prove it, he hoisted her thighs up over his arms, lifted her hips and rocked into her with such stunning power that they both cried out at his entry. Then with every swift claim of her body, he panted with every ram of his powerful hips. She arched into him and dug her nails into his waist.

His teeth bared. His eyes narrowed. And closed.

She strained to get nearer to him and have him bury himself ever more deeply inside her.

"This," he seethed as he slammed into her in a sultry rhythm, "this is what you should have. Not him. Me!"

Triumph left her speechless as tears of delight slid from her eyes.

He pummeled her with delicious need long denied. She felt his madness in very bone of her body and hung on to him for the unmatched glory of it. His thick cock pounded into her, stretching her and giving her the rapture that swept her along on a rolling wave of pleasure. She raced with him to a savage summit and on the precipice; she hung suspended for a pulsing moment until the two of them floated to the earth.

He curled her close. Stroked her back as she murmured her pleasure and nestled nearer.

"Come to bed, *mon amour*. You were in the rain today and must not become ill." He stood and hurriedly stepped out of his breeches. He tugged her to her feet and led her to the bed.

Upon the mattress, he pushed her down, laid her out and hovered over her. "Christ, a lush beauty. How I have wanted you like this. Naked and mine." He traced his fingertips over her, kissing what he touched and praising every part. "Your brows. Fine and straight. Your eyes. Large and penetrating. Your throat. A swan's. Your breasts. Ah, a sumptuous prize for your lover, *ma cherie.*"

She shifted as he sucked her nipples and she sought to find his cock and stroke him. Even now, his shaft was long as her hand and firm.

"Careful, my pet. You tempt me too much and I will force myself on you again."

"Well you know that was not force, Etienne. It was a declaration we have needed from each other for years." She opened her thighs that he might be invited to sink inside her and feel her words to be true. "What I wish from you again as soon as you are up and once more able."

He choked in laughter. "Tempt me, will you?"

She lifted her chin.

"We shall see, then." His fingers delved inside her and parted her. "You are plump and wet. So ready to have me again." He clutched her close, his fingers stroking her, making her arch and offer a wanton picture to him. "I cannot let you go to him. I'll find a way to stop you."

"Make love to me once more and I will re-consider," she bargained with him.

"Witch," he joked, but sank to her body to nibble at her, lick her to soft cries and pleas for more.

She offered up herself as if she lost all awareness to his love, his care.

He kissed her and stroked her as though she were the finest and last sustenance he would ever claim. His devotion had her mewling for release.

"If you do not have me, I shall scream the house down, you awful man!"

He reared up, raised her legs and draped them around his shoulder, then rammed her with the fury of his love. In seconds, he had her hanging on that same precipice she discovered minutes before, then took her to a frantic place where she moaned her delight.

He kept up his incessant seductive rhythm, driving hard as she bit her lip to keep from wak-ing every one from here to Rome. They dissolved together.

Rolling to his side, he took her with him.

She was whimpering, her body pulsing. "Don't leave me. Here, I need you," she said as she took his hand and kissed it. "Oh, *mon Dieu*, Etienne."

"Sweet," he said and held her close to him, a tight clutch that alarmed her for its ferocity. "You are a woman ripe for love. Mine. And long I knew it."

Exhausted, replete, she caressed the line of his cheek. He'd leave her again and soon. She had to think quickly. Act it too. "There well might be a way to catch our culprits without me going to Giorgio's bed."

Etienne arched a brow and caught her finger between his teeth. Then he bit her.

"You are a madman," she exclaimed. "Give me that!"

He nipped her again.

"I see. You want to know how, eh?"

He sucked on her finger in a sensuous apology, then let her go. "Tell me, you nagging woman."

"This afternoon, as I descended the stairs I saw a man talking to Giorgio in the drawing room."

"Yes, and?"

"They argued."

Etienne frowned. "About what?"

"I was not close enough to hear."

"And this is of interest to us in our quest?"

"*Oui*. Because the man who spoke with him is a servant."

Etienne scowled. "Odd. We always suspected one of James's official staff was the informer, not a servant. So then, who is this?"

"Wonderful question."

"Why?"

She grinned. "Earlier, I went below stairs and asked who among the staff speaks Italian."

"Ah. I see. You will drag this out, won't you, darling?"

In the darkness, she flowed near to him and hugged him to her. "I love having you close to me, *mon amour*. Why would I not tell you all my secrets in the tiniest increments?"

He sighed and chuckled, his fingers skimming her shoulders in an adoring caress. "Indeed. A sin to make any haste with your skin to mine. Hell, what sweet torture this is. But it ends. The sun dawns. The British Navy itches to find Murat and his ragtag fleet. We need only capture the remaining spy in this city and in your cousin's household. No rush. None at all."

She pinched his waist.

"Ouch!" He wrestled her to her back, his thighs parting her own, the tip of his cock probing the entrance to her very ready body. "Tell me who it is, my darling, and I shall attempt to make you the happiest woman in Naples."

She giggled and tipped up her hips to receive his marvelously erect shaft deep inside her needy body. "Thomas, the footman, who is, by the by, half Italian and half English."

"Very good, my sweet." Etienne rewarded her with the full possession of her body. "Any other suspects?"

She licked her lips in sheer delight. "Yes, I had to rely on James to tell me this bit of news. I had to ask him, you realize, because I didn't want to leave the job half done, rely on only one source and such. So. *Viola!* It seems that Quinn, our butler speaks the local language also."

"How expert you are, my sweet spy," he murmured as he fully engaged himself inside her and had her sighing at his expert thrust. At once, he began a slow, sure drive that sent her rapidly up, up, up to a thrilling completion soon matched by his own.

Minutes later, as they lay still in each other's arms, Etienne told her what they must do now.

"Tomorrow you will concoct a means to have the footman overhear how you have discovered the identity of the traitor in this house."

"Only the footman?"

"We must test each suspect, one at a time. We shall see if he reacts. If he runs to Giorgio or someone else. Leave it all to me."

"But what then do you suggest I do to flush out the loyalties of the butler?"

"Wait. Let me work my way. If the footman is not our mark, we will take the other."

"This piecemeal method makes me uneasy."

He kissed her forehead. "Do not fear. We will not fail."

She hugged him fiercely. "I count on it. I do not want to end my years at the beck and call of the Home Office." She glanced up at him, eager to press him for all he might give. He'd made love to her completely risking the possibility that she might carry his child. Didn't that imply he must be hopeful of a future for them? "I want Bony gone, and you and I to have a new life."

His fingers threaded through her long curls. "In France, everything may be gone. Your *chateau* and mine. Our friends, certainly. Our farmers."

"I am not gone, *mon amour*," she told him with joy in her heart for what they had claimed here these past two nights in Naples. "I am here because you saved me from the mob and from Bonaparte's agent."

"I vowed to your father when we were imprisoned in the *Conciergerie* to save you from the guillotine, Solange. That was a fourteen-year-old's bravado and rash hope to escape. If it looked like chivalry or valor, it became so only in the proof."

"If he knew what you do now for France, my dear *Monsieur Noir*, he would be grateful and utterly proud."

"What I did then, what I promised him, I did for survival. What I do now for England, I do for justice. But what I do today to free you from this Italian rascal, I do because I care for you, Solange."

Her heart dropped. He could not bring himself to declare more than that he merely cared for her?

At her distress, *Noir* rolled away from her and dressed. Once more at the balcony doors, he glanced back at her.

Tonight, it was he who said goodbye. "*Adieu*, Solange."

Adieu, mon coeur.

Chapter Five

October 6, 1815

Solange descended the staircase, intending to visit with James in his office. She rarely ventured there, but this morning was different. She and he had concocted this plan yesterday, immediately after she had visited below stairs. After both of them had shared vital information about the servants, James vowed to aid her. He had never questioned her methods—and always praised her results. He had given her carte blanche ever since she identified a ring of Norman smugglers on the London docks a few years ago. In league with a member of Parliament, the ring had been selling British naval secrets to one of Bonaparte's agents holed up in Dover. She had broken them after trailing the M.P. and watching him accept money from two of them one night outside Almack's.

She knocked at James's door. There was no answer. She tried again. And turned the latch. She flinched. It was locked.

"Quinn?" She called down the hall for the butler.

He appeared almost at once. "Ma'am, May I help you?"

Solange turned toward the butler, who of late always seemed so readily at her beck and call. "Is Lord Moreland in his office?"

"I assume so, Madam. He usually is at this hour."

"James?" She called through the door and rattled the knob. "I must speak with you."

The butler stood there with her, befuddled by the locked door, it seemed, as much as she.

But then she heard footsteps across the floor, the fiddling with the lock and saw the portal open wide to her. "Good morning, James. I must speak with you."

Her cousin, a tall, slim graying gentleman, was usually calm. His visage this morning was stiff with tension. His blue eyes dim. His brows knit. "Come in, do, Solange. Quinn, good you are here. Call Tom for me, will you? I need him."

"Yes, milord. Straight away, sir. Might I be of some assistance at the moment?"

"No, thank you. Do send Tom." At that, James swept aside for Solange to enter his domain and promptly shut the door behind him. When he was on the other side of the room and he and she had taken the wing chairs near the fire, he continued. "That went well."

She nodded, the game afoot as it were and she in her element. Cool, eagle-eyed and patient.

"How is Cora this morning?" He asked, apropos of nothing for this meeting save absorbing time as they waited to execute their plan to trap the footman. "Maryanne said she sent you her own maid to serve you."

"She did and Hettie is a fine substitute. She says Cora has a fever now and is laid very low."

"Hettie seems a good girl," he said, his voice trailing off, troubled.

"She's been kind to Cora in her illness. She and Cora share a room upstairs," Solange ventured, glancing at the clock now about to strike nine.

"I did not know," James replied, his brooding gaze on the door.

"So much we do not know about our servants, *oui*?"

He skewered her with a jaundiced look. "How true. First my naval adjutant. Now my servants? The house is a vipers' nest."

She smiled sadly. Given any other circumstances, she would have openly laughed. But James felt savaged by her latest news that one of his household might be in arms with the French upstart Murat. "My dear, you must not take all the blame for what's occurred here. It is your situation in the midst of transition from the French to us and now the new king of Naples wants the upper hand. Chaos draws them to you. So many loyalties. So many dashed hopes. All over Europe, I dare say."

"It will take us centuries to recover from the ravages that little Corsican has cast upon us," he said with bitterness.

"Bonaparte stepped in to the void of the Terror and charmed so many," she said with a sigh and a wave of her hand. "Liberty, equality and fraternity."

"And ruthless tyranny," James added. "Fortune hunters, all of them."

She smoothed her skirts. "The Bourbons did not govern well in France. They too were ruthless, suppressing the peasants to the benefit of the nobles."

"I thank god you escaped the rabble, Solange. You were innocent."

"And Papa? Was he?" Her ire always too bright when speaking of the Terror, she tempered it and ran a hand over her brow. "I was too young to really understand what the situation was, James. I recall we ate well, dressed in silks, danced..."

"Your parents did not deserve to die in that manner."

Never in the twenty-two years she had known her cousin had he ever been able to say the word 'guillotine'. Perhaps because his own mother, had been visiting her sister, Solange's mother, that summer in Nevers, and escaped Robespierre and the scaffold because she was married to an Englishman.

"No, they did not," she agreed. "No one does."

"Will you return to your home?"

She inhaled sharply and stared at him. Save for last night when she spoke of it with Etienne, she had never thought of it as more than a fantasy. "I might. If it seems safe. Now that that ghoul Fouché is no longer minister of police, it may be."

James shook his head in derision. "He and Talleyrand have nine lives, working for the king, then the republic, then Bonaparte. I'm shocked the new king reinstated him. So many died at his order. It may well be safer for you to go back because the new king has promised all émigrés a return of their lands and titles."

"Ah, *oui*. If they have never cooperated with Bonaparte or the Committee of Public Safety—and so many did. To save their lives, they bowed to that horrid little man."

"The Allies have assured no violence. Why don't you go? Make peace for yourself."

She gave him a small smile. "If that is possible." *If Etienne comes with me.*

There was a rap on the door.

"Come!" James called as he checked Solange's eyes.

Tom appeared before them. "My lord, you wished for me?"

"I do, Tom. Rearrange the wood in the fireplace. It does not burn well. Plus I have made a glorious mess of my desk this morning what with all the dispatches from Admiral Wentworth. Do take the whole of it and burn it, will you."

Tom widened his large almond eyes, his gaze skipping to the expanse of his master's desk. "Of course, milord."

As he stepped to remove the grate and picked up the irons, Solange attempted to see his hands. Alas, she could not detect if he had a tattoo. Sighing, she nodded at James and began their little drama. "I have success with Prince D'Oro."

The footman, Solange noted immediately, pricked his ears at the word 'success' but continued about his duties.

"Oh? How so?" James asked her.

"He has asked to court me and I have agreed."

"I am not surprised at his suit, but astonished you accepted him," James said to play his part. "He was devoted to you the evening of the Mask. He has been a widower for some years, I understand. "

"He may come to speak to you and ask for permission."

James sniffed. "A little arcane, don't you think, given your age and status as a widow?"

"Well, my dear," she said, laughing, "thirty is not that old! But I wish you to stall him."

"Whatever for? If you like him—"

She cringed for the benefit of Tom who glanced up now and then from his work. "I like him quite well and could care for him more. But I have little time for courtship, James. You know I must finish my work for you," she offered with wry implication and a fretful wringing of her hands.

"As soon as you find your bird among those in the nest, you are free to do as you wish."

"Thank you, James. I will detect him soon, I know. I ask you to bear with me."

"I do. But speed is essential. Murat sails nearer to Naples every day, so says Wentworth in the Bay out there." James tipped his head toward the city's port.

"Never fear!" Solange got to her feet and stepped over to kiss her cousin on the cheek. "Thank you for your help with the prince. I will test my *tendre* for him before I commit to marriage. Trust me, I shall be more settled once we hear Bonaparte is safely tucked into the south Atlantic on that god forsaken island."

"Quite so, my dear."

"I'm off to visit my seamstress," she told him with a wink. "Home in time to help Maryanne with the baby and then change for dinner."

"And if the Prince calls round for you?" James asked like a doting father, as the two of them put on a show for the benefit of Tom.

"Invite him to dinner!" she joked.

"Dearest, he is such a bore. I'd sooner jump naked into the Bay."

"Hardly suitable activity for the stuffy English ambassador."

"Off with you!" He shooed her away. "Your seamstress awaits! Tom, do finish there, will you? I'm up to visit with my wife for a few minutes."

Solange arrived home after two o'clock. The sky drab, the wind brisk, the horrid weather had only added to her tension. She entered the front door, smiling politely to Quinn as he helped her divest herself of her pelisse.

"A good afternoon, Madam." The butler looked serene, nothing amiss.

She peeled off her gloves and handed them to him. "Has Lady Moreland taken luncheon already?"

"Yes, ma'am. Would you like a tray or care to dine in the small parlor?"

"A tray in my room, thank you. Send Hettie with it, will you?" She did not wish to see Tom.

She wished only to know if he had stolen any of the false documents from James's desk and left the house to take them to a contact.

At that, she headed toward the stairs up to her suite. She fretted, pondering whether to seek out James for news. To inject herself into her cousin's office once more today would be unprecedented. She had either to wait for him to find her and tell her if their ploy had worked or simply wait until they gathered in the drawing room before dinner.

"Lady Starling," the butler called to her as he emerged from the cloak room off the foyer. In his hand was a white box with pink ribbon. "This came for you a few minutes ago."

From *Noir*. She took it, eager to read his well-penned note. "Thank you, Quinn. Did the same urchin deliver it?" *One should take care to note such details.*

"I doubt he was same boy as the previous two, but he was a scrawny piece."

Hurrying up the stairway, she shook the box and anticipated its contents. Another chemise? Made of what? Its card conveying good news or bad?

Inside her suite, she sank back against the door and thought better of venturing out today.

She had stayed away as long as she could, but the storms off the sea matched her morose mood. She pushed away and made her way through her sitting room to her bedroom and paused. There, upon her deal table sat another package. Similarly wrapped in white silk with pink ribbons.

She smiled.

She frowned. Why two packages today?

What was amiss?

Putting the first box down in one chair, she rushed to the newest package and pulled it open. Within the satin interior lay a long pair of ivory stockings. She gasped in astonishment at the sight. The stockings were thigh high beauties topped by a ribbon of Point d'Alençon lace. From the town of the same name in central France, the stockings were stunningly delicate, yet heavy, hand worked. Were they difficult to acquire here in a city so recently under the French control of Murat? Perhaps not. She held the pair up to the light from the far balcony windows and marveled at the craftsmanship by makers who continued a technique developed in the tiny town more than four centuries ago. Then she saw the other element about this gift that made her frown.

She sank down into the nearest chair, pondering this gift's differences from her first two. The French lace. Stockings. And now here was a third difference. A note of vellum sat in the bottom of the box. The stock of the paper was not cream but ivory. The paper was not folded but a sheet. And the words in a large black script she did not recognize made her read the paper twice. "The garden at midnight."

Someone knocked on her door.

A hand upon the stockings, she gave permission for the person to enter.

Hettie stood on the threshold. "Milady, I came to tell ye your luncheon will be up soon as Mrs. Brown can rustle it up. She went on an errand and only just returned." Her eyes drifted to the open box and she smiled. "You got your package. Good."

"When did it arrive, Hettie?"

"I brought it up meself. Noon, I'd say. Noon."

"How did it come?"

"Come?"

"Was it delivered by the same boy who brought the others? Did Quinn say?"

"Oh, no, ma'am. No. Pretty stockings." She peered at the white lace and grinned. But when

Solange did not respond, the maid blinked. "I'll get your tray."

"Yes, thank you."

Hettie had not precisely answered her question, had she? And the woman's nerves were a tad raw, weren't they?

Solange inhaled deeply. Her gaze traveled to the gift in the chair. The box Quinn had handed over. At once, Solange noticed that Hettie would not have seen this one from her vantage point at the doorway.

Snatching it up, Solange strode with it into her dressing room, then soundly closed the door and threw the latch. She tore it open, its wrappings falling to the floor. This present, too, had her catching her breath.

The garment was a chemise. Sheer white muslin, exotic, erotic. Meant for a paramour or a well-loved wife. The lace trim on the *en coeur* bodice of this garment, she also recognized. It was fine point from Ragusa near Venice, an area which had cast out Napoleon more than a year ago. This punto, she noted as she held it up to her torso, was like the previous two chemises in that it would fit her. *Noir*, it seems, had an eye for her and her healthy proportions long before he appeared before her in the garden at the Mask. Though she smiled at the thought of his ability to order a garment to precisely fit her, she brushed aside the euphoria and bent to search for the note.

This one was of the same sturdy vellum. Cream colored. Heavy stock. Folded in half.

She flipped it open.

The script was big, bold, black.

'My dearest Bella. Wear this for me tonight. Maid in Ragusa, it pales beside your beauty. Yours, M.'

Long. Verbose even, compared to the other notes.

Still.

She knew this one was from *Noir*. All signs pointed to it. The script. His handwriting. Even the "M" she understood. But his mistaking of the English word 'maid' for 'made' was unlike him. He was better educated than to make such a silly mistake. So it was none. He'd had his reasons for the substitution.

Then too, why should she have two gifts today?

She would think on that this afternoon and analyze possible answers.

One thing was certain. Tonight at midnight in the garden she would most definitely learn. She

prayed *Noir* came to visit her before she had to keep her rendezvous with a careless French spy.

Chapter Six

October 6, 1815

A deluge of rain pummeled the house. Solange sat, conversing and laughing with
Maryanne and James at dinner, and hoped for a
break in the miserable weather. If Solange went
out to meet anyone tonight in the garden, she
would not only be soaked but considered de-
ranged. She ate hardly any of the roast beef. She
drank far too much wine. By the time James
wanted his brandy and cigar, Solange wanted her
room, her solitude and some more definitive
word of what, if anything Etienne had learned
today about Tom's loyalties and the reason for
the mistakes *Noir* 'maid' in his note. She certainly could not do other than suspect he meant
Hettie, given the woman's odd behavior this afternoon. That and the fact that Quinn did not
recall another package being sent to her today

made her look at Hettie with more interest than before.

Solange put down her serviette by her plate and addressed Maryanne and James. "I really am quite done in. I hope you do not mind that I retire."

Maryanne, true to her nature, was agreeable. And so Solange made her way from the dining room up to her suite.

Hettie was putting out upon her bed her woolen robe and a flannel nightgown.

"Thank you, Hettie." Solange had hidden the Ragusa-trimmed chemise, its wrappings and note in her chiffonier. That piece was the only furniture in her room which had a lock. Distrusting Hettie, Solange thought it prudent to hide the chemise away along with the note that accompanied it. "You are wise to put these out for me."

"On a night like this, I didn't think you'd want one of them sheer gowns you wear."

Cora must have told Hettie of this, for how else would she know? "Right you are."

"I saw your stockings, milady. A lovely gift, it is." She inclined her head toward the pair of hose that still rested in the gift box. And when Solange only nodded at her statement, she rushed onward. "May I bring you anything, m'am? A toddy? A nip of spirits?"

"No, thank you. Unlace me and then you may leave me for the evening." She presented her back to the maid and as she worked, Solange opened a topic of conversation. "How is Cora?"

"Better, yes, ma'am. Up and about tomorrow, most likely."

The maid sounded anxious. Wonderful. Not used to skullduggery? "Please tell her I wish her a speedy recovery."

"I will, mum." She reached to help Solange off with her gown.

"No, you may go. I'll do the rest myself. I'm eager to be alone."

"If you wish." Frowning, she curtsied. "Anything else, ma'am?"

"No. Thank you." Solange waved her off with a flutter of her fingers and a dismissive smile. "Good night."

"Night, milady."

The door closed with a click.

"Dear god," a bass voice echoed around the bedroom as a tall figure in black stepped from the draperies at the balcony doors. "I thought she would never leave!"

Solange laughed, overjoyed like a girl at his appearance after such a dreadful day. Then she ran to him. "Forget her. Kiss me." But when she grasped his great coat, she clung to him, her body alive and warming to his nearness as it always did. His mouth told her he found solace in her as well. With a hand to her nape, he ravished her mouth with his lips and tongue and teeth, until the urge to do more had her leading him toward her bed.

"Wait, Solange. I am a muddy mess."

Suddenly aware of his state, she tore at his coat. "Sodden! How long have you been here?"

"Too damn long," he muttered as she peeled off his wet coat. "That girl is a pest. She has puttered about here and there. I could not see her every move, behind the curtains as I was, but I do believe you should check your jewelry, *ma cherie*." He chuckled as Solange stripped him of stock, waistcoat and shirt, then caught her back to embrace her tightly. "I have missed you, Solange."

The insistence in his eyes and the feel of his solid body, warm and reassuring, against hers had her complying. She wound her arms around him and opened to his possession. Tonight he moved in a fluid leisure she had not had from him those other nights. His measured pace thrilled her and soothed her testy nerves. He took her mouth with command, his tongue deeply stroking the cavern within. His lips skimmed the corner of her mouth, blessing her there and on her chin, the hollow of her throat and the tops of her breasts.

"You wear too many clothes." His hands pushed down her gown to puddle on the floor. Disregarding it, he pulled her close, his hands drifting along her undergarments to cup her *derriere*. His fingers gathered up her petticoat so that his hand caressed her thigh and squeezed. "I feared for you today. Here. Inside. Alone. Before when you were threatened, I have been with you."

"You are with me, Etienne. You keep me safe." She breathed deeply, losing her head and her balance as his fingers caressed her hips and her inner thigh to delve into entrance to her body.

"I'd keep you always, if I could. You must know that," he insisted, his mouth hot against her cheek.

That he denied them any future tore at her composure. But she would not deny them both what was needed at this moment. She tore away

her petticoat and raising her arms to have him strip her of the rich chemise he'd given her. Then she walked backward to her bed, leading him by the hand. "The ills of tomorrow are nothing here."

In a thrice, he pushed her backward, her legs caught at the knees by the mattress. She undid his flies with a speed she enjoyed and found his cock, long and ready to fill her. But this once, she had to taste him, measure him, please him in a new way. She pushed him over and bent to him. Her mouth encompassed him. As he groaned and plunged a hand into her curls, she took him totally in her mouth and laved him, tip to root and back again.

She heard him grind his teeth and as she plied him with the wet rasp of her tongue, she rejoiced that she could so delight him. So many years they had hungered to enjoy each other and she would not hurry now.

But he rose up and pressed a fingertip to the corner of her lips. "Solange, sweet. Hold. Allow me the final moment."

In a heartbeat, he rolled her to the bed and thrust inside her. Filling her, commanding her, he took her to those new and glorious edges of the universe where she clung to him. He pounded into her and the moments they had been apart were reduced to ashes of the past. In their place was this fierce rippling sensation of wild reciprocated love.

"How can it be I misjudged you?" he asked after the two of them lay more fully on the bed, arms about each other, luxuriating in their naked abandon.

"You thought me a dried up prune of a widow?" she confronted him with the worst of what he might have thought.

"I thought that marriage to George Starling may have soured you on bedsport."

She widened her eyes at him. "Why so?"

"He was such a bully boy. All pomp and bluster."

"No substance," she confirmed.

"Forgive me, darling girl." With careful fingers, he combed her hair upon the pillows. "I concluded you were a marvelous actress as you enchanted men. A woman who had not known a real man's love in her bed and therefore, incapable."

She snorted. "Odd, then that you could think me capable to attract the men I have done."

"How true."

"I do like men." She traced a fingertip along his square jaw.

"I thought so."

"Not all men," she clarified.

"Thank heaven."

"I am particular."

"And I am grateful," he told her as he sank to push her breasts together and thrill her with his hot lavish kisses.

This largesse was more than she had gained from him the previous two nights. And it set her to wonder at its cause. What had they gained today to free him of his reticence to love her totally?

Best to persuade him with the weapons she had at hand. She opened her thighs, found his very interested cock with one hand and stroked him. "Come love me, my man. My gratitude comes when you are inside me."

She showed it to him then in abundance and had them both panting, perspiring upon her sheets.

Naked, she rose to pour water from her pitcher for them both. She brought the cup to him. "Drink. You need it. The first we have shared in a long time."

The words, unplanned, brought back unbidden memories of his similar ones to her so long ago as they ran together to escape mobs. "'Drink,' he'd urged her along their escape route from Paris whenever they'd found water or wine. 'You need it. The last we will have for a long time.'"

He took her cup from her hand now, his dark eyes holding hers as he drank. Then handed it back to her and beckoned her. "Come here to be warm."

Another set of words from long ago.

She smiled slowly at him, climbed upon the bed and nestled to his incomparable human comfort. Was she spoiled, demanding, impertinent to wish it to continue? Forever. "Tell me what you saw today."

He sighed, his breath upon her brow. "No man left this house today."

"Not any one?"

"No. Only your maid there." He tipped his head toward the door.

"Hettie?"

"If that's her name."

Solange sat up and stared into the void of night. "A woman. Reading your note about a 'maid', I thought it possible one was a spy, but I can scarce believe it."

"Why? You are a woman. Capable of espionage."

"Yes," she agreed. "But I have motivations. What does Hettie have?"

"Greed?" *Noir* tossed off the possibility. "Money? Lust?"

"Lust? Hettie and Tom? Hmm. Possible," she mused.

"Or Hettie and Giorgio–?" *Noir* speculated.

"Oh, my!" She was nigh unto apoplectic at the mere idea of such two mismatched people in bed with each other. "*Mon cher*, I hardly think–"

"Strange bedfellows and all that, you know."

She wrinkled her nose.

Noir nodded. "I do know the Prince likes blondes. He's had three mistresses with pale hair."

Solange frowned. "Blondes? Really?"

"Yes."

"But–"

He became intractable, shaking his head at her. "I know it was your maid who left the house. No mistaking her. She's thin and wore the house livery, black and red. She came out of the kitchen door, below stairs. It was not your cousin's wife. I know her red hair. It was not your cook. She is short, with meat on her bones. This woman was young and blonde and–"

"Blonde. *Mon Dieu*." Solange put two fingers to his lips. "Get dressed."

"What?"

"Come with me." She slid off the bed and searched for her robe.

"Solange. *Un moment, s'il vous plait*. Where do you want me to go?"

She pulled on her garment, then rummaged through her *bombe* trunk, digging to the bottom for the one item she needed for such a night as this. Long, deadly, sharp. "Above stairs."

"Listen to me, Solange. I do not wish to take her into custody just yet. We know she spoke with Giorgio and gave him a sack filled with papers."

Her stiletto firmly in her grasp, she slipped it into the deep pocket of her dressing robe. "Papers? From James's desktop?"

"We may assume so. One of my men witnessed Giorgio leave his own house within minutes of your maid's departure."

"And where did he go?"

"A farm on the coastal road south toward Calabria. The man he met is one of Murat's agents, well known to us."

"So Giorgio is in league with them," she concluded.

"I would say so. I have a man following him. Meanwhile, I do not wish to take Tom or the maid lest they have others they wish to inform."

"But you are here with me and both of them could escape–"

"They cannot. Before I crawled up your tree limbs to your balcony, darling, I posted four men around the house to monitor. No one leaves here tonight without me knowing who it is."

Her heartbeat slowed. He was totally in command of the situation and she beamed at him. "Very wise of you to surround the house. This means no one leaves and no one enters."

At her playful tone, *Noir* blinked, then studied the ceiling. "But of course. So tell me, does someone enter tonight?"

She nodded, wiggling her brows. "The garden. At midnight."

"I see." He crossed his arms. "And might we have any idea who this is?"

Solange put a finger in the air. "A superb question!"

He wrinkled his brow in exasperation. "Solange–"

She quickly explained about the arrival of her new stockings, the note and her conclusions about Hettie's innocence and Cora's guilt. "So you see, you are absolutely right. We will not go to get the maid. We wait for midnight."

"And then we three will go to the garden."

"Three?"

"Me, you and that sharp little tool in your pocket?"

"Of course. " She beamed at him, caressing the handle of the stilletto.

A slow smile of triumph spread across his handsome face. "Take off your robe, my darling. We have another hour to enjoy together before we descend to your soggy garden."

She gleefully let the robe drift to the carpet and climbed up next to him. "How can I be so fortunate?"

"Your answer lies here." He kissed her with a sweet seduction of his lips that tasted and lingered and tested. "And here," he whispered as he plied his skillful way with her along her throat to the valley between her breasts. There, he devoted himself for long moments to her nipples, laving them, shaping them to hard high points with the warm ministrations of his mouth. "Here, too." He sank between her thighs where he kissed her and caressed her, enticing her to open to his lips, his tongue and his avid appetite.

He murmured tender phrases in French, all of his need for her. She longed to memorize the words, recall the phrasings, the tone and tenor of his delayed passion. But his dedication to her engulfed her senses, swamping her mind with his rich passion.

He tended to her like a man who had long planned his seduction. She hurried him not at all until at last she knew the urge toward completion that would not be delayed or denied.

She arched up against him, her arms binding him to her, the knowledge that this might be the very last time she might enjoy him driving her to chain him to her if she could.

"Etienne," she crooned his name as he rocked them both in joyous thrusts. Completing her as she had never been with any one else, she rejoiced and feared to part from him. "I love you. You must know this. I love you."

He buried his face in her shoulder, his lips silently moving on her skin. Holding back words of love or devotion? She would never know. For he rode his own storm to completion at that point and collapsed upon her, rolling to his side and taking her into his embrace for silent minutes.

As her body cooled, Solange came to herself. He had not told her he loved her. She must face that. Find a way to accept it later. Much later. His reasons? She might never know. But the way he had made love to her? Ah. Her woman's instinct said he cared. Poor man, wrapped in his own demands, he could not break from them to see beyond them. She counted herself fortunate—and yes, indeed, loved—that he had been able to share his body with her, if not his heart.

Realist that she was, she would take what he had given, treasure it and grieve later the loss of what he might not be capable of giving.

At a few minutes before the midnight hour, the two of them descended the dark staircase. Shoes in hand, they tiptoed through the main floor and round to the receiving room and to the doors to the garden terrace. As planned, *Noir* left her to take took the back stairs down to the servants living quarters and emerge to the garden from there. Solange strolled out along the terrace alone. Surveying the shadows among the cypresses and lemon trees, she made her way to the entrance to the maze and took a seat upon the small stone bench where a few evenings ago she had sat with Prince Giorgio. The thought of his treachery made her shiver in anger and she pulled her shawl higher around her throat. In her right hand, she concealed her sharp knife and held it ready to strike.

The rain, thank heavens, ended an hour or so ago. The salty sea air mingled with the fragrances of rosemary and yew. Minutes passed. One. Two. More....

A twig snapped.

At once, a dark figure appeared before her. Wearing trousers, like a man. With a scarf upon his head, like a woman.

Solange stood slowly. She would not frighten this creature, but lure him closer. Whoever he was....

He pushed a pistol barrel into her stomach.

Precisely what she had wanted. Solange struck. Up into the man's guts. Once. Twice.

He grunted. Staggered.

Right behind him came *Noir* who plucked the intruder up by his collar. "Do not accost the lady, sir! This way with you."

Noir began to frog-march the gasping man toward the servants' kitchen.

Solange waylaid him. "I struck him, *Noir*. He must be quite wounded."

The man grabbed *Noir's* arm, stumbling to his knees in the wet grass. *Noir* laid him out, removed Solange's knife and pushed off the scarf. "Dear lord, Solange. This is—"

"The cook?" Solange could scarce believe her eyes. "Mrs. Brown? Why?"

"Money. They paid me." The stocky cook grimaced, licked her lips and grabbed at her bleeding stomach. "I took a chance, but you..."

Solange ignored her words. "And Tom and Cora? Why did they help you?"

The woman raised her florid face to Solange. "Money speaks, don' it?"

"And for taking it," *Noir* told her, "they'll hang for treason."

Chapter Seven

April 10, 1816

Nevers, France

"Stop the coach," Solange told her driver when the team of four had rounded the edge of the forest where once one might have glimpsed the *Chateau de Bussy-Nevers*. Her eyes closed, she bit her lips and questioned once again the wisdom of her journey. She had no need to be here. She needed not a home or land or income from tenants. Her parents were dead. The servants gone. The peasants most likely living quite peacefully without any intercession from her. But James and Maryanne had kept at her after all of them returned to London before Christmas.

"You have no occupation," James had repeated. This of course was true since Napoleon seemed safely tucked onto a miserable little dot in the south Atlantic. Her days of espionage were done. By circumstance and definitely by choice.

"You lack color," Maryanne had pushed her. "Try the French air. Even Paris. Why not? I understand the social life is oh so charming and you know many attached to the new court. King Louis would welcome the Princess of Nevers. Think how you could sail among them. That Starling Woman. I bristle with delight at the approbation, dearest. You would have men at your feet, as here you do."

Exactly. As if Solange had a desire for any of them. Save one man whom she expected not to see and had not since that night when they had routed all the spies in James's household.

She opened her eyes and upon the tapestry walls of her coach, she saw his face, his hair, his eyes, his lips as he bid her *adieu*. "Good bye, my darling Solange." He had taken her into his strong demanding arms as the sun rose that fateful morning, and she had hung there, furious at his departure when all seemed solved, resolved, and ending well. Except for their relationship. From that, he would leave once more to god knew where. His eternal work for England. To hell with espionage. If she ever met the head of Home Office, Special Operations again, she might stab him for his infernal need to run spy rings and use men like her precious *Noir* until he dropped of treachery or despair.

But of course, she had met the master of all spies again at a dinner only two weeks ago. And she had not killed him, though she skewered him with questions about *Noir*. The man told her *Noir* was safe. He was still working, yes. Where? Well, my dear lady, I can only say he is happy on the Continent.

Happy, was he?

She would bloody well see about that.

If she could find him and she did ask all along the way from Calais here if anyone knew of his whereabouts. A few said they might have seen him near Montmorency, north of Paris, but she doubted he would return there. Ever.

Still, she could not flush him out. Alas, the man was not only elusive, he seemed invisible.

And so she had to try to learn to live without any hope of seeing him again. After all, Napoleon was removed. The radicals of the Revolution were dead. Perhaps *Noir* would not be able to rid his blood of the need for *revanche* or justice, or whatever he termed his devotion to his craft.

The only thing left for her to do was rectify the horrors of her childhood by building a tranquil life as she advanced, god help her, to her dotage.

"*Madame, pardon e moi*," the coachman called down from his box, "May I continue?"

"*Oui, Monsieur, s'il vous plait.*" *I keep you from your task. I keep myself from the future. And that, I have never done. Never.*

She turned at once. Her view out the window, over the pale green valley gave her a glimpse of gentle willows swaying in the breeze. Her jaw dropped.

This was not what she remembered. This chateau, buttery and golden against the pale blue sky, with fat circular turrets, the moat wide, the water within dancing in the rays of the sun. The trees grew tall, green and healthy, reaching to heaven. The peasants' homes stood here and there in the valley. Cows grazed. Sheep, too. A dog barked and ran toward a child.

This was not what she remembered. She pushed away the images of snarling men, grasping women, a man in short trousers who struck her father with his pitchfork, a woman who dragged her mother to a cart, pulling at her hair.

Solange put a hand to the coach strap to catch herself from doubling over. She breathed deeply, forcing back bile as she had that day when the enraged mob handed her parents and her over to the Paris Committee and took them off to Paris in a filthy cart and interned them in the Conciergerie.

"*Madame*?" The coachman bent over her, having opened the door. "Are you ill? I'll fetch the constable." He ran inside the open double gates to the front door of this chateau that resembled no edifice she recalled. All here had changed so much in twenty-three years.

Sitting as if she'd taken root here, she watched an older man hurry out the door, the coachman right behind him.

"*Madame*?" the older fellow stuck his bald head inside the coach and stared at her as if she were the Madonna. "Oh, *Madame*! *Madame*! It is you!" He took her hand and tugged at her. "Do come. Come now. We have waited for you for so very long."

"You have?" She stepped down the coach steps and to the well-manicured pebbled drive. "I am sorry. But you are...? Do I know you? You seem to know me, but I am at a loss." *And I am also babbling like a brook.*

"*Oui, Madame*. I am Gaspard. Louis Gaspard. No? No memory of me? My father was in service to your own. We are the family of your chamberlains."

She stared at him, at once on guard that he or his father may have been among those who helped to send her parents to their doom.

"Ah. I see your problem. Natural, I would think. My family left and went south with your governess, the butler and cook. We have lived together until last year when new King Louis said all of you might return. We thought if you did, we might be of service to you again."

"But how could you hope? How could you even know I was alive?" *How and why would you care?*

His grey eyes twinkled. "We have known you live in England. Our mayor told us."

"Your mayor," she repeated, overcome at the kindly reception.

"He knows everyone! And when we returned, he told us he had word of you, your health, your marriage. But you lost your husband, eh?" Now the man rattled on in his delight and his enthusiasm was contagious.

"Yes, I did. Many years ago, I must add. I am a widow."

"Ah, *oui*. We hear of you. That Starling Woman."

She feigned delight. "How wonderful my reputation precedes me."

"It does. It does! You caught a few spies."

"A few, yes."

"Well, but to us, you are our *Petite Princesse*. I will get Paul to take your trunk to your suite. And we do have a maid for you. Charmaine. My daughter. She is young, unpracticed, but she wants to please."

"I see. Thank you. But how do you–?" She paused to absorb how ordered and fresh everything looked. True, the furnishings were sparse. Had the mobs hacked them up? Did she remember that? She shook her head. But the house was clean. The tile floors spotless. No dust upon the sideboard.

She looked at Gaspard. "How do you live here?"

He arched a brow and shrugged. "After the king decreed we could move back and you and all émigrés could come, too, we have lived here without a challenge. Those in the town and the valley knew we were your servants and did not dispute it. And as for the house? It was empty. We cleaned it. White-washed the walls. Straightened this and that. Made it as best we might. At least, the radicals had not burned it down. They did take torches to so many."

"Yes." She had seen many a charred spectre along the road from Calais. "I am delighted, too." And she was. She most definitely was! She clasped her hands in a rush of excitement. She had not expected this. Not this bright renewal. "Will you show me the house?"

"*Oui, Madame.*" He seemed surprised at that, his glance drifting up the grand blue marble staircase and fluttering back down to her. "Now?"

"Now."

She saw the reception room and recalled how the chandelier, now gone, had glowed with hundreds of candles when once her parents had hosted a ball. She viewed the state dining room where the mahogany table for forty survived and so did the rose and gold *Sevres* china her mother adored. She viewed the drawing rooms, both formal and family, and noted how the upholstery had faded to a frosted blue. She glimpsed the huge kitchen where she met Gaspard's wife, Lucille, who bobbed and muttered her joy to have her home again.

Home. Well. Was it?

"The private suites are in better condition, *Madame*. Shall we?" He indicated they climb the master staircase.

She nodded, pausing at the landing to crush her urge to cry at the sight of the full length portrait of her grandfather in court regalia. "Startling that survived."

"*Oui*, we were surprised at that. You must know though there is more."

She questioned him with an arch of her brow.

"Your mother"s portrait is here," Gaspard said with whispered reverence. "Your father's, too."

"No! Where?"

"We have them in the nursery. The paintings need repair. A few gashes from knives, I am sorry to say."

"But we have them!" she exclaimed, as they reached the top of the landing. "Where is the nursery?" She asked in a pique. She should not have forgotten where she spent most of her days here. But the child in her had demanded she forget the pain of the past.

"This way." He turned left and took her down the gallery to the far end of the house. He opened the door to the musty, unused room, which sans furniture and drapes, was still bright.

She passed him and walked straight toward the life-size portraits of the man and woman who had dimmed so much in her memory that she was ashamed and startled at her feeble mind. How tall her father had been and quite handsome. Dark, curly hair. Rose cheeks. His eyes startling silver. *Like my own. And my mother?*

Solange moved to stand before the lady who stood, smiling out at her, her lips generous and kind. *Maman. They hurt you. Beat you, too, like they did him.*

She dashed back tears from her cheeks, willing herself to stand there until the beauty that had been her mother destroyed the images of those who had destroyed it. How had she forgotten that?

"You were a child."

Chapter Eight

"You were a child." She knew the words, felt them sink into her bones. Yet how long it took her to realize they were not her own thoughts but pronouncements by a man whose voice she knew well, she could not say.

But she felt him draw near. His footsteps on the parquet floor, his warmth behind her, his hands upon the points of her shoulders.

When he led her to rest back against his chest, she closed her eyes and this time, she willed herself to drive out the ugliness that had shaped her childhood.

He hugged her to him, his lips in her hair. "Welcome home, *ma cherie.*"

She spun in his arms, her own winding about his waist. Here in the sunshine, she saw intricate elements about him that had escaped her for years and years. He was truly dark of eye and dark of hair. His jaw was sturdy. His cheekbones sharply arched, the hollows deep. His nose aquiline. His lips. Oh dear. His lips were the most beautiful feature of his chiseled face. They were wide and lush, almost too beautiful to belong to a man but oh so beguiling. But she would not surrender to his charms. Too many months stood between them. Too many explanations must come her way. His departure from her life in Naples had crippled her severely and she had spent the intervening days rallying herself from a despair she at times thought never to escape.

"Tell me how you are here."

"I came as you. In a coach."

She cursed roundly.

He chuckled, but his eyes were sad, sympathetic. "Welcome me to your home, *ma Petite Princesse*. I have longed to be with you again."

"How can you say that?" She grew angrier.

"It's true."

"It's simple. You wounded me, leaving me as you did that morning in Naples. And no word from you in all these months."

"You can be difficult," he complained with a strained smile.

"Difficult? Oh, you cannot even imagine how difficult I can be."

"But I can. I have seen you wield a knife and I've no wish to be on the receiving end."

He would make light of this? How dare he? Had he no understanding of her fright for him? Her care? Her love? How could he not? He was a wise and crafty man. "Oh! You know what I mean! Why are you here? How? When? Speak quickly so that I—"

He picked her up and tossed her over his shoulder. Hanging as she was, she could beat upon the two fine cheeks of his de*rriere*. This thrilled her, of course, for two firm reasons, but she kept it up incessantly as he strode down the gallery and headed into another room.

And there he tossed her onto a bed.

"You are a savage!" she said as she flopped on the mattress, watching him go, and realizing she was in a fabulously appointed boudoir, with huge bed, two dressers, mirrors, a large coppered bath and giant armoire.

He chuckled. "You make me so!"

"You must come here." She beckoned him with two hands, the fresh paint of the walls filling her eyes and the smell of it refreshing her nostrils. The joyous fact that he was indeed here with her and in a very fine bedroom filled her with childish hope. She knew enough from past experience with him to temper her expectations of anything he might do to show her his

affections. "Satisfy me as to why you are here."
And tell me how long you stay.

"I've come to show you a few things I have purchased."

"What?"

He moved to the far corner where he disappeared behind her mother's tall jade and pearl Chinoiserie folding screen. "Before I came south, I was in Paris for a few weeks. While I was there," he said as he emerged, his hands full of ladies garment boxes, "I ordered a few items."

Pressing her lips together to stifle the urge to take his gifts and rip open the gorgeous pink and purple and cream wrappings, she sat upright and asked him to explain the more pertinent issues of his whereabouts. "How long were you in Paris?"

"Since January," he tossed off with a blithe grin and stacked his gifts upon the bed.

"Why?"

"I went to bend a knee to Louis."

His cousin. Wise to go. Wise to do it. "And did he welcome you back into his fold?"

"Indeed he did, my pet." He sat beside her on the bed. "Even offered me my place at court."

"Did you accept him?"

"One does not refuse the King of France. He also offered me a role to serve him as I did the Home Office."

As a spy for the French crown? "What did you say?"

"I do not want a job that has me fawning over him. My father did that for his brother and paid with his life."

Relief surged through her.

"But I do want my rights to my lands."

"And he gave you those?"

'He did. How could he not? In light of my service to his cause. Removed, as it was, from this country in service to the British."

"You served so many well," she praised him and took his hand. "Me, foremost among them."

He raised her hand and kissed her fingertips. "At your service, *ma Petite Princesse*."

She inclined her head. "*Monsieur le Duc de Montmorency*, I am pleased to make your acquaintance."

His face lost the mask of gaiety. His eyes searched hers. "You have known me best of anyone."

"I agree. A man of duty and honor. Even as a boy of fourteen. Where would I be without you, my duke? Not here." She waved a hand to denote the room. "Not alive. Not capable of thanking you once more for your service to me. I assume you have helped with all of this restoration?"

"No, *Madame*. You would be wrong in that. I arrived here only five days ago. It is your chamberlain and his family who have made the *chateau* livable once more. Thank them not me."

"I will. But then you must tell me why you came five days ago."

His mouth spread in a wide grin. "James wrote to me to tell me you had decided to return."

"James! I thought you two were not on the friendliest of terms. You could not even enter the house in Naples lest—"

"That changed after you and I caught Mrs. Brown and Tom and Cora at their worst. James and I became friendly while I was in London giving evidence against the three conspirators."

Solange jumped to her feet. "You have been in London? When?"

He winced. "After the new year. I remained for a few weeks."

"And you did not call upon us? Me?" She was raving mad. "How could you be there and not come to see me? After what we were to each other. Knowing how I care. How?"

"Solange, *mon amour*—"

Tears cascaded down her cheeks. She clenched her hands, then pointed to the door. "Get out!"

He shot up and took her by the wrists. "Listen to me."

"What could you say? What could you ever say to me that would be worth my time?" She tore away from him and strode like a lunatic to the door. "Leave me."

"No." He blocked her, braced his legs wide and folded his arms.

"Fine! I will leave!" She side-stepped him but he caught her about the waist and hoisted her in his arms.

"You are troublesome when you feel rejected," he murmured, not struggling in the least with her weight or the fact that she pummeled him on the chest. But when he dumped her on the bed and climbed atop her, thighs across her own and pinned her to the bed, she bucked to be free. "I am not letting you go, so struggle all you wish, you remain with me."

"Oh, you are the most infuriating man," she accused him, unable to even look at him, torn open by his delay to see her, his damnable objectivity and her declaration of despair of life without him.

"Will you babble on, or will you listen to me now?"

She pouted and quit her opposition. "Hurry up about it."

"Look at me."

"I know what you look like. Tell me things I don't know."

He sighed, but did not release his grip or his position. "That morning when I left you in Naples, I did so in haste because I had to speak with the admiral in the Bay about the three traitors. He told me they suspected that Murat and his fleet headed for a landing south in Calabria. I had to go to relay word to the king of Naples' forces."

She did look up at Etienne then because she knew what had happened to Murat. "They caught him as he landed the next day. Because of your swift action, I presume."

"Yes, and shot him in a firing squad five days later."

"His death meant all of Napoleon's allies in Europe were at long last conquered," she added. "And where did you go after that?"

"I handed over the three traitors to the admiralty and made my way back to London via coach. On the road outside of Paris, I had my driver take me north to Montmorency."

She could tell by the haunted look in his eyes that what he had seen was not pleasant.

"The chateau was razed. The stones dot the grounds, the walls stand like ghosts to the past. But the villagers welcomed me home. Some recognized me by my resemblance to my father."

"Etienne," she whispered. "I am so sorry."

"Don't be. I loathed that house."

Her mouth opened. She was without words at his confession.

He stared at her, but saw only a wretched past. "My mother and father hated each other. No, you did not know. How could you? Why would you? I never said. Never wanted to remember. I accept that the house is no more. If it were, I would not live there."

He paused, his gaze flowing over her face, his attention totally on her once more. Still she anticipated he wanted to say more.

"I want to build a new house. Not as it was, but anew. Open, airy. Grand. A testament to the future. What do you think?"

His mood was now light, whimsical and she felt his desire for a matching humor. She smiled at him. "I believe that is a marvelous idea."

"I want a life, Solange. I want a different existence. I want peace and boredom."

She chuckled. "Etienne, you will never be bored. You will always do engaging work."

"I want to farm."

"Farm?" Now she thought he might be daft.

"I want to read and walk in my wheat fields. I want to watch hens lay eggs and sheep have lambs."

"Darling, I think you will need more than that to amuse you."

"I want to celebrate Christmas and my birthday. I want to watch the sunrise and the sunset."

He was quite serious. And in a small corner of her heart, she felt a novel hope blossom.

He leaned close to her, his lips a whisper from her own. "I want my home filled with people, guests, servants, and children. I want a wife I love, the one woman I have adored for all my life."

She dared not breathe. To listen to this and not have this promise of life with him be hers would kill her.

"Solange, *ma petite*, I love you with all my heart. Marry me. Let us begin anew, make a life we can enjoy every minute of our days. Marry me, will you please?"

She raised up and put her lips to his. "I have loved you forever. Never another."

"As I have loved you, *mon amour*. Marry me."

"*Oui, Monsieur Noir. Etienne. Oui.*"

She kissed him then, once, twice, a thousand more times.

Then he rose from the bed and went to shut the bedroom door. His dark eyes dancing in need, he sat down beside her and told her to open the boxes.

Aching for the moment they would become one in this bed, she quickly rose and tore at the wrappings. "From Paris."

"Ah, Chantilly lace! A chemise I do not have in my wardrobe," she said and nodded at him with glee.

"The next one."

She tore at the wrappings. "A petticoat? How lovely. Sheer. Scandalous, is it not, my darling?"

"Silk from worms in Brussels. You will wear this petticoat only for me at home."

"And this one?" She lifted another gift and shook it. "What can this be?"

He nodded. "Open it."

She could only grin at the sight of the black stockings, lace etching the top. "Alencon?"

"*Oui, Madame.* Only for you and only from your fiancé."

She wound her arms around his shoulders and beckoned him down with her to the comfort of the bed. "I shall wear them all for you."

He wiggled his brows. "Let's remove your gown, shall we?"

"And I'll don all three so that you may amuse us both and take them off."

"No. I would see the stockings." His onyx eyes turned languid with desire. "Only the stockings."

He helped her remove her gown and her underclothes, then sat beside her on the bed. As she gathered up the stockings and slid them over her ankles and up her calves, he smoothed his hands over the silk and his lips followed. "Solange, my love, no woman is as lovely, as brave or bold as you. I will love you until the day I die and most likely afterward because you

are more exquisite than lace, stronger than silk, stronger and more resilient than any woman I have ever known."

As he entered her, she welcomed him to his new existence as her lover, her husband and the man who would purchase far too much lingerie in the next forty years or more.

THE END

Bonus Feature!
HER BEGUILING BUTLER
Delightful Doings
in Dudley Crescent, Book #1
By
Cerise DeLand

www.cerisedeland.com

Published by W. J. Power

ISBN: 978-0-9908943-0-8

Her Beguiling Butler

A lady shouldn't desire her butler. But what's a woman to do when the man fascinates her? She must taste him...or dismiss him.

And how does a man kill his scandalous desire to kiss his charming employer? Especially when he must protect her from an unknown villain...as well as his dastardly need to possess her.

LADY STARLING'S STOCKINGS

Excerpt of

Her Beguiling Butler

January 17, 1820

No. 10 Dudley Crescent

London

"Finnley, please," Alicia addressed her butler with a shaking hand to her brow. "I am perfectly fine. Really I am."

The towering creature had her by the forearm, half carrying, half dragging her toward the foyer bench. Slamming the front door to her townhouse, too. "You fell on the doorstep, my lady."

"The ice," she explained, gasping, her hand to her chest where something inside hurt badly.

"I told Grimes to melt the ice and sweep it all away. I shall dismiss him," her Goliath told her.

"No, don't!" she begged him because she liked the young footman. But she was gazing at her butler's fabulous face and so she tripped on the edge of the carpet.

"Madam!" He caught her.

"Oh, Finnley!" Alicia gasped as the giant swept her up into the power of his arms.

Was she inclined to trip on ice? And carpets? Last week, she'd inadvertently stepped on broken glass in the upstairs hall outside the door to her bedroom suite. She'd asked the maids about how the vase broke but no one claimed knowledge. "Honestly, Finnley. No need for this. I *am* fine."

She was not. Not at all. Her knees hurt like the devil and the balls of her hands smarted. And being held like a bit of china by this man who'd begun work only last month was unsettling. Unnerving. *Endearing.*

"No, madam, you are not fine," her man shot back as he plunked her in the oversized wooden seat which was where he usually sat while waiting to receive or dismiss her guests. Reaching up, he pulled the bell. "I'll get a maid. You look like the very devil."

"Really, Finnley." She had enough sense in her to chastise him for his blue language, even if she secretly admired his forthrightness—and his scrumptious mouth. "I only need to sit here a minute and catch my breath."

He scowled at her as he went to his knees before her. Those pale blue eyes, the color of a clear June sky, locked on her own. "If you are well, my lady, why do you clutch one hand to your bosom?"

"My chest hurts, Finnley," she told him on a whisper. At least she hadn't succumbed to the sob that filled her throat. To cry before him—this creature who seemed so impervious to weather or emotions—would be demeaning.

Alarm flashed in his cool countenance. He took her hands from her chest. "Where?"

"Right—" She pointed to a spot beneath her right breast, enough toward her breast bone that she didn't blush when she indicated its location. "Here."

He looked down and considered the swell of her bosom in her red redingote. "Sit back."

She loved the way he dwelled on her overly generous curves. "What?"

He pushed her to the rear of the seat, her derriere sliding along the polished wood. "Let's remove your coat."

She pushed his hands away from the frog clo-sures at her throat. The heat of his big hands was enough to unsettle her, rouse her, make her breasts...*honestly!*...tingle. "I can do this."

But she fumbled. And frowned.

He pushed her hands to her lap. "Don't be a ninny."

She snapped her gaze on his.

"I apologize," he said with the first humor she'd seen gracing those lips. "Let me do this, madam."

She sighed and fell back against the hard wood. The firm mahogany countered the rising desire that shot from her belly upward. Swal-lowing hard, she shut her eyes and scolded herself for this outlandish attraction she bore her new butler. *Madness at first sight, it was.* She sighed at her foolishness to desire a man she barely knew and a servant at that!

She jostled as he undid her coat and spread the wool wide across her shoulders.

"Let me help you off with this," he said, so solicitously that it brought frustrated tears to her eyes. Her departed husband, a scoundrel whom she assumed would never rest anywhere in peace, had never assisted her in removing her clothes. Unless he had wished to have her naked. But that had been for only a few minutes while he did his duty by her and departed for his own suite.

"Of course," she said, relishing the service of this man whom she'd hired last month on good references from the Earl of Newport. She'd never met Newport though her husband had known the earl and liked him. That aside, to be quite honest, she hired Finnley for other qualities that recommended him to her.

She smiled to herself and admired the butler's ministrations while he tugged her coat from her arms and gently urged it over her fingertips.

No, she had not hired Wallace Finnley for the fine words Newport had written about him. Frankly, rebelliously, deliberately, she'd hired him for his brash looks. Not quite handsome, he was a collection of first-rate attributes that made her mouth water. The coal black hair. The cold blue eyes. The jaw that defied one and all to argue with him. The height, towering. The breadth, oh so comforting. The very sight of him each morning in his fitted black uniform made her catch her breath and hold it until her heartbeat resumed normal rhythms.

Which now it definitely did not.

Finnley remained much too close. And his eyes roamed the front of her. *Yes.*

He considered her bodice where she was certain her chest heaved. Her cleavage where her overlarge bosom displayed a deep divide. Where her flesh hardened at his appraisal and her nipples peaked and pushed at her chemise.

And chafed her.

She cleared her throat.

"Let me test to learn if you've broken a rib."

"Test?"

Yes." His icy gaze froze her own. "We can call a physician if you like and he—"

"No. I detest doctors." She'd had enough of the charlatans when her husband took ill more than a year ago and died within the month.

"Fine. I can determine if you're hurt badly. Sit forward. Arms up a bit like this." He raised his own in demonstration.

She imitated him.

He put his hands to her waist. They were so big, so hot, his fingers so damn long that she swore he could span her entire waistline. But the delicious warmth of his touch set her swooning...and she caught herself. Smiling at him, she winced when he pressed on either side of her ribcage. "Does that hurt?"

How could it when his strength rippled through her? "No."

He slid his hands higher at her sides. "This?"

She shook her head and licked her lips. *Oh, my.* His thumbs rested beneath the wealth of her breasts. And her lower body flooded with a surging tide that had her blinking like a flustered debutante.

"Does it?"

"What?"

"Hurt?"

"No, no."

His hands drifted higher and he pushed against the sides of her breasts so that they thrust forward like two ripe melons against the bodice of her gown. "This?"

"That?" She squeaked at him.

He glanced down, his thumbs a bare half inch from her nipples. His pressure was firm, but gentle.

Her heartbeat was fast, but insistent. Her mind went blank and then, her gaze met his.

"That doesn't hurt, does it?" he asked, his bass voice, usually of such bold timbre that she could hear him in the hall, on the stairs or greeting her callers. But now his voice held only a fraction of its own resonance.

She considered his mouth. His wide, sculpted lips that spoke of order and precision.

"No," she told him with as much normality as she could summon. "There is no pain." *But something else...*

She put a hand to his and squeezed it. His skin was supple, hot and—

He dropped his hands.

She sagged. Her interlude was ended.

"You've not broken a rib. Thank God."

"How do you know?" She searched his face.

"If you had, you would have screamed when I pressed your brea— your chest just now. You've badly bruised yourself in your fall."

"Good to know. But...how do you know that?"

He shrugged. "My father was a medical man. Not trained. But helpful to the tenants in our village."

She tipped her head, curious at his words. Often when he spoke, he seemed to be obtuse, his phrases veiled as if he were other than he was. *Why did she think that?*

"Here's the maid," he said to her as if she needed a reminder of where they were and what they were about. "Mabel, do go to the cellar and fetch us a bucket of ice. A few towels. Long strips of cloth to make bandage rolls."

"Finnley," Alicia said, her voice strange even to herself. "I don't need ice."

"You will. I saw you fall, my lady. If I hadn't caught you, you would have hit your face. Broken your nose. Your teeth. Don't be polite with me. I know that your knees must be bruised."

"Do you think so?" she asked him in a daze. Was it the nearness of him or her injuries that fogged her brain? To break the spell, she wiggled, and yes, *dammit*, her knees did pain her. Her shins. Her arms, too.

"Allow me, madam."

The next second, her butler of one month, this veritable mountain of a delicious man, had pushed up her skirts. They draped, bunched up like limp lettuce, over her thighs and her bare knees were quite throbbingly black and blue and very, very large.

She clamped a hand to her mouth and let out a whimper.

"Don't worry, my dea— my lady," he said. His hands cupped her calves, stroked her skin and soothed her worried mind. He winced at the sight of her injuries, then looked sideways at the maid. "Mabel! That ice bucket! *Now*!"

"Aye, Mr. Finnley." She turned tail and sailed off.

My dear. Had he attempted to call her his *dear*? Alicia allowed her delight to curl her lips and to counter that, because it was not appropriate to grin at any endearments from one's butler, she set her teeth.

"Let me unlace your boots."

She didn't answer. There was no need. In her heart, she agreed that he could and so why not enjoy the stroke of his hands on her calves and her ankles? The power of him as he tugged off, one by one, her dainty wet boots was soothing. The delicious release was tantalizing as he took her stocking feet in his hands and massaged her chilled and weary little toes.

"That's wonderful," she crooned, going with the pulse of his touch.

He made some gravelly noise in the base of his throat.

Yes. That was the way she felt, too. *Primal.*

"Ahem," she said and sat taller in the chair...but only because she should.

"I'm afraid you are going to have a terrible time walking." His eyes were on her bare knees. "We'll take it slowly. Where is that girl with the ice?"

"She'll come, Finnley. Don't be impatient."

"The longer we wait, my lady, the greater your disability."

"Surely, you are mistaken. I can bend my kn—" She tried it and gasped. Then dropped her leg, her foot to the tile. "I stand...or rather, *sit* corrected."

"You'll be fine. Now let's see." He bent over her knees, his face so close his breath fanned her fevered, swollen skin. "I wonder if you've broken any bones. Shall I touch you?"

"Dear man," she said much too quickly for propriety, "you already have!"

His cool eyes turned to blue flames. "I'll be gentle."

"I'm certain."

"I'll be brief."

"Oh, don't be."

He tilted his head as if to ask precisely of what they spoke.

She cocked a brow at him, aware and un-ashamed of what they did speak. But she had to camouflage that, didn't she? Propriety was such a dictator. "Do as you must, Finnley."

He put his hands to one of her shins and pressed along her bone. She was tender but nothing stuck out as if it were broken. "I doubt you have suffered more than a bad bruise."

"Thank you. I hope so."

"Here is the maid," he said to Alicia as tenderly as he touched her. But to Mabel, he barked, "Where have you been?"

"Had to go to the cellar, sir, to get ice. Had to break it up, too, I did."

"Fine, fine." He put his fingers to Alicia's shin and she wanted to cry joyful tears at his exquisite finesse. Then he stood and stared down at her. "You're going to bed."

"A good idea." She put her hands to the bench to stand and yelled out when she put pressure on her palms.

"Enough of that," he said and scooped her up into his arms, heading for the grand staircase.

She surrendered to him. He was officious like any butler but his air of authority belied servitude. His very stance exuded power. His words demanded compliance...except when he looked and spoke to her.

He surveyed her now with that smoldering interest that melted her to the core. "Follow me up, Mabel. Bring all that with you."

Alicia relaxed in Finnley's embrace, reveling in his solicitous behavior. The heat, the comfort, the rapture of being held by such a powerful creature flowed through her like good red wine.

And to think, it was her butler, her servant, who did this to her when her husband had never elicited any naughty thoughts. Nor had any of her suitors during her Season. Sad, that. And many had called her a beauty.

"You must let me walk," she told him for the sake of the maid and her own decorum. Her arm around his shoulder, she clung to him.

"Nonsense."

He kept on up the stairs.

Grinning, she rejoiced in his stubbornness. "I appreciate your dedication, Finnley."

He glanced at her, his gaze hard blue sky. Then he smiled. And his expression spoke of more than duty or kindness. It spoke of fondness and laughter.

Her insight was but a flash.

His long black lashes flickered as he turned away. "You are welcome, my lady. Let us not speak of it again."

Who is Cerise DeLand?

Cerise DeLand loves to write about dashing heroes and the sassy women they adore. Whether she's penning historical romances or contemporaries, she's praised for her poetic elegance and accuracy of detail.

An award-winning author of more than 50 novels, she's been published since 1991 by Pocket Books, St. Martin's Press, Kensington and independent presses. Her books have been monthly selections of the Doubleday Book Club and the Mystery Guild. Plus she's won rave reviews from *Romantic Times*, *Affair de Coeur*, *Publisher's Weekly* and more.

To research, she's dived into the oldest texts and dustiest library shelves. She's also traveled abroad, trusty notebook and pen in hand, to visit the chateaux and country homes she loves to people with her own imaginary characters.

And at home every day? She loves to cook, hates to dust, goes swimming at least once a week and tries (desperately) to grow vegetables in her backyard in south Texas!

More Novels by Cerise DeLand

Regencies

Lady Starling's Stockings

The Stanhope Challenge,
Regency Quartet, box set

Regency Romp Series:
Lady Varney's Risque Business, #1
Rendezvous with a Duke, #2
Masquerade with a Marquess, #3
Interlude with a Baron, #4

Delightful Doings in Dudley Crescent Series:
Her Beguiling Butler, #1
His Tempting Governess, #2, *debuts Fall 2017*
His Naughty Maid, #3, *debuts Winter 2017*

Erotic Regencies:
His Delectable Cook
Sense and Sensibility

Victorian Romances
Those Notorious Americans, Series:
Wild Lily, #1, *debuts October 2017*

Daring Widow, *debuts Winter 2017-2018*
Scandalous Miss, *debuts Spring 2018*
Outrageous Countess, *late 2018*
Charming Roué, *late 2018*

Medievals
Swords of Passion Series:
At Her Service, #1
For Her Honor, #2
With Her Kiss, #3
* * *

Military Romances
7 Brides for 7 SEALs Series:
You Were Always Mine, #1
No Getting Over You, #2
Only You, #3, *debuting 2017*

SEALs Going Hot, box set
Burning for Nero
Conquering Zeus
A Long Time Comin'
Hard Drivin' Man

Contemporaries
Tall, Hard and Trouble, box set

Tall, Hard and Mine, box set,
Coming Soon!

Tall, Hard and Fierce, box set,
Coming Soon!
***

Visit Cerise's website:

http://www.cerisedeland.com